SAL

SAL

MICK KITSON

CANONGATE

Published in Great Britain in 2018 by Canongate Books Ltd,
14 High Street, Edinburgh EH1 1TE

canongate.co.uk

1

British Library Cataloguing-in-Publication Data
A catalogue record for this book is available on
request from the British Library

ISBN 978 1 78689 187 7
Export ISBN 978 1 78689 188 4

Typeset in Bembo by Palimpsest Book Production Ltd,
Falkirk, Stirlingshire

Printed and bound in Great Britain by Clays Ltd, St Ives plc.

MIX
Paper from
responsible sources
FSC
www.fsc.org   FSC® C018072

To my parents, Babs and Terry Kitson

Chapter One

Snares

Peppa said 'Cold' and then she went quiet for a bit. And then she said 'Cold Sal. I'm cold.' Her voice was low and quiet and whispery. Not like normal. I started to worry she had hypothermia. I saw a thing about how it makes you go all slow and quiet. So I felt down and her back was warm and her belly was warm. Then she went 'Stop lezzin us – ya paedo.' And then I knew she didn't have hypothermia.

But it was cold. The coldest night since we came here. I knew the wind had turned to the north from my compass and the shelter faced southeast because west is the prevailing wind here. So the wind was coming in the top where we'd laid on the spruce branches. Peppa didn't have a hat. I was going to make her one once we'd snared rabbits. But I hadn't put the snares out yet. I pulled off my hat and pushed it down onto her head.

'Is that better?' I whispered in her little ear. But she'd gone back to sleep. I was awake now and I started worrying for a bit. I used to time worrying by the clock on my phone. I did ten minutes most mornings, but it had gone up in the past few weeks because there was a lot to work out and plan before we ran. I was going to guess the time. I could feel it was nearly dawn. There was no light but I could feel something. I can nearly always tell what time it is. I don't know how but it used to be important to know it. Because for instance Maw and Robert used to come back at just after 11.00, and after I'd fitted the lock on Peppa's door I used to make sure it was locked and she was inside asleep just before they got back.

They didn't even know I put the lock on it. Didn't know I'd nicked a mini drill-driver and two chisels from B&Q. I snipped the alarm tags off with a nail clipper. I bought a sash lock in the big ASDA and watched five YouTube videos before I fitted it. They didn't even notice the wee holes I drilled for the key, the paint on the doors in our flat was all scuffed and knocked anyway. Then Peppa had the key. Robert couldn't get in if he tried. He never tried. If I'd put a lock on my door Robert would have kicked it in and woken Peppa. He wouldn't have woken Maw because when she was drunk and she passed out you couldn't wake her.

And he hadn't started going in Peppa's room then but I knew he would soon because he said he would and Peppa was ten and that was when he started on me.

So I thought I'd have ten minutes worrying. I knew it would start getting light soon. In the SAS Survival Handbook it says you should make a body-length fire along a lean-to shelter and then build a barrier behind it from sticks to reflect the heat. I hadn't done that yet because I wasn't sure this was where we were staying just then. But it was alright. It was a little flat raised bit above the burn and there were big birches all around. We'd tied the tarp up to two of them to make the shelter. The tarp was camouflage brown and beige and bits of yellowy white like for deserts. But it worked because I ran back away from it into the wood and looked down between the trees and you couldn't see it.

Except you knew someone was there because I could hear Peppa yelling 'Sal . . . come and get a look at this!' It was a toad and she stroked it and I said 'It's poison on its back to stop predators eating it.'

And she said 'I'm not going to eat it Sal. Can you eat it? I don't want to eat it. I'm gonna build it a house.' And then she made a little house out of flat stones and pebbles and put the toad in it. She said it was called Connor after a boy she liked at school.

I worried about fire and people seeing it, not so much in the day but at night. If your wood's dry there isn't a lot of smoke from a small pyramid fire, it's just smoky if the wood is wet or too new. And also the wind blows it away. And also we were in the Last Great Wilderness in the UK and we were exactly eight miles from the nearest human habitation and roughly four miles from a forestry track and five miles from a road. I chose this place very carefully using an Ordnance Survey map I nicked from the library where they have all the Ordnance Survey maps of the British Isles. We were exactly half a mile into the forest behind a ridge that runs up towards the top where it is just under 3,000 feet. In fact another twenty-eight feet and it would be a Munro and there would be all climbers and wankers in cagoules going up it.

There are no trees at the top but according to the map there is a stone circle. The hill is called something in Gaelic and when I asked Mrs Kerr she said it was pronounced Magna Bra. Magna Bra. I told Peppa and she wanted to go there because I told her Magna means big in Latin and she was delighted and skipped about going 'Big Bra . . . big bra'. She is a dirty-minded wee bastard and she wants to watch her swearing.

But at night you could see the fire glow from a way off. Not on the tarp side but on the other side. So I thought if I build the barrier they talk about in the handbook it would block the light at night from the east. I don't know what way they'd come if they came out here and looked for us but they might come from the east. The motorway is east of us and they'd use that if they came out here. But I don't see how they can or how they'll know we are here.

I decided after my worry to make the barrier today and then set snares. We had got enough food for another two days I thought. Or three if I don't eat and Peppa does. So we needed to start trapping and hunting. I had Robert's airgun. It was short and you pump it up. It shot .22 pellets and I got two tins of them. I wouldn't let Peppa use it yet in case she shot herself or me by accident. But I am a good shot. I practised in the hall of the flat and I worked out the way to adjust the sight for the parabellum at longer ranges. I watched a YouTube video about it too, three days before we left. On seven pumps it can go through a bit of 9mm plywood. I brought it there in a zip-up hockey stick case I found in the school changing rooms.

It was getting light. In October here, that means it was just about 7.20 a.m. Peppa slept on in the bag and I hauled myself out so as not to wake her. The leaves that had fallen were light yellow and they shone as the daylight came through the trees. The birch trees shone too. Birch is white and it would be good for the barrier because white reflects light and heat. I blew the embers back and fed in some little sticks with burny ends. I'd put a stack to dry on a flat stone overnight too, and once it took I built a pyramid over it. It hissed and smoked and I got the steel frame and put it over and then put the little kettle on it to boil. We had teabags and UHT milk and sugar in tubes from McDonald's. Loads of them.

The sun was up now and it was bright through the trees and steam was lifting off the wood floor in little white wisps. There were wee sparkles of frost on the leaf edges and twigs and the wind had dropped so the smoke went straight up between the trees. It was still, just the wissshh sound of the fire. Then I could hear birds and squawks of crows. Nothing else. No rumble of a road or traffic or wheels. No banging or bleeping. No telly. Nobody shouting.

I had four snares made from twisted wire with little gold rings where the wire made a noose and green cord to a wooden peg with a notch in it. You set them in runs where rabbits went and left them overnight. I had seen it done on YouTube on a survival site. It looked easy and the rabbit was dead when you went back. But I wouldn't mind killing one. I had never killed one. Or anything apart from Robert.

It said you should bury them for a few hours to get human smell off them, so I scraped back the leaves and got them out of Peppa's backpack and covered them up. I bought them in a fishing tackle shop in town with the money I got from one of Robert's cards. Robert always had cards when he came back from wherever he went off to. I used to nick them when he was asleep drunk.

The thing about Maw and Robert was they never noticed anything. If something changed or moved they didn't even know. I knew where everything was in my room and the rest of the flat. I knew how many cups we had, how many spoons. I knew how much milk there was and how much washing-up liquid. I noted it all the time. I'd done it from a baby. I noticed what things were and where they were and I noticed when they moved or changed or went. Maw and Robert didn't see anything.

Maw was worst. Even her cans – she never knew how many she had left. I did. I used to hide them and she'd not even notice there were only two instead of three in the fridge. Sometimes if she just had two she was alright. I noticed that years before so I'd hide a couple and just leave her two and when she came round and wanted one I'd say you've only got two left. And she'd go, I thought I had a four-pack, and I'd go, you must've drunk them. And she'd say aye. When Peppa started nicking her fags she didn't notice either.

Robert noticed nothing either, because he was mostly drunk or on weed or both, and even though he stared really hard and long at things he never noticed if something was missing or if I'd moved something or bought something. Robert's eyes were always half closed like he was squinting and they were always red from weed and bevvy. The little bit of the white you could see was yellow.

The tarp and the hunting knife and the kettle frame and even Peppa's walking trainers all came in the post, all got on Amazon and all with the nicked cards Robert brought back with him and kept in the bedside drawer. I was careful when I was nicking the cards or lifting his wallet. Once he was out of it, lying on the sofa, and I tried to pull it out of his back pocket and he half woke up and grabbed me and went 'I'll cut your fucking hands aff' and then he flopped back asleep and I got it then.

The only thing he did keep his eye on was me. 'Alright ma darlin'?' he used to say. He once said I was his daughter to a guy in the chippy. I wanted to say 'Ah'm fuckin not' but he was giving it the big man and had his arm around my shoulders and going 'This is ma lassie Sal.' If I'd said anything he'd make it worse later so I just shut up and stared at the guy.

Peppa woke up and said 'Is Connor still there Sal?' And I went over and lifted the stone on his house. And he was.

It was nice and damp under there for him in the leaves and muck. Peppa said 'Brilliant!' and jumped out of the sleeping bag and started putting on her shoes. They were £84 on Amazon and they've got Vibram soles which are the best for walking and climbing.

Peppa can run faster than anyone in the world I think. She has got really long legs and she looks like wind running along. She was faster than any boy at school, even boys older than her. In fact she does everything fast. She is either still like a stone or going really fast. She eats fast and she talks fast.

And Peppa will eat anything, and she is ALWAYS hungry. When we were wee, we were hungry a lot because Maw was out or drunk or we had no money and Peppa used to go to other flats round the close and ask for food. She learned to eat anything, not like most kids who hate salad and only want chips.

But Peppa used to beg chips at the chippy and ask kids at school for food. And teachers. And in the end I told her to stop and I had to get her food because if they told, the social would come round and take us. The social took kids all the time and they always split them up. So I didn't say anything to anyone and Maw warned us we'd get took and split up. So I nicked food for her a lot, and I got her bags of salad and carrots and once some beetroot in a plastic bag that was cooked and she loved it, and she stopped begging food and nobody told the social on us.

And when Robert started on me he said if I told, even if I told Maw, we'd get took and split up. He said Peppa would get fostered and adopted by Africans because she is half an African and I'd get adopted by old people and we wouldn't be together. And that is never going to happen.

So it is good for surviving if you will eat anything like

Peppa, but not if you are hungry all the time like her. And she said 'Ah'm starving Sal' and I gave her some Dundee cake and four belVita biscuits and I said 'We're gonna snare rabbits' and she said 'To eat?' and I said 'Aye', and she said 'Good.'

She had a look at Connor under the stones and picked him up and he sat in her hand and she talked to him. She told him her name and my name and where we came from and why we were in the woods. Then she put him back in his house and got her Helly Hansen on.

Rabbits don't hibernate and there are loads in the Galloway forest and they mostly live in warrens at the foot of hills and slopes where there is scrubby ground cover and grass. Grass is the thing they eat most and not carrots or lettuce like Peter Rabbit on the telly. It was autumn and most sites said they would be active and you had to look for runs in the grass to set the snares. I had never set a snare or gutted a rabbit or skinned one but I had seen it done loads of times on YouTube.

I got the snares out from the leaves and mud and put them in the pocket of my coat. I had my knife in a sheath on my belt.

We walked down from our shelter along the burn and climbed over it on rocks and then up a slope where the trees were thinner and there was grass and ferns. Peppa ran. The ferns were turning brown but they still stuck up high and she was lost in them and then I'd see her red hair shoot by in a gap. I watched the ground looking for runs. There were paths there made by animals and I saw prints of deer in the mud and other prints I needed to check later in the SAS Survival Handbook. We walked up until it came level and then beyond was another long slope down towards the loch right at the bottom. Peppa tore down the slope and I wanted to stop her from frightening anything but when she was running like that you couldn't stop her. I had seen her tear away like that before, leaping over logs and fern stumps, running and swift and smooth like she was on wheels. Then she stopped dead halfway down and shouted 'Sal!'

I came down towards her where the trees had thinned out, mostly old birch and oak, some with big branches thicker than me that hung down to the grass. She was by a big grey rock that poked up out of the grass. And she was pointing down in front of it. 'Look' she said.

It was rabbit holes, three of them with droppings all around. And when I looked I saw more, some of them were further back up towards an oak tree and the holes were covered by fringes of grass. There were nine of them in total, some were disused with no droppings and some had fresh dark mud in piles outside where they had been digging out. I could see runs going away from the holes, little lighter-coloured dents running along in the grass. They mostly went down the slope towards the loch. The further you got down the greener and thicker the grass got and less trees and ferns.

'It's a warren' I said.

'Set the snares then' said Peppa.

'You can't set snares by the warren, they'll go round them. Bear Grylls said you have to walk away from the warren along a run and set the snares away.'

'I saw that one Sal and he didn't even get one! He had to buy a rabbit to cook. Wanker' she said.

She was right but he still knows what he is on about because he was in the SAS and he has survived everywhere and he jumps into bogs and frozen lakes even if he doesn't need to. But he is a wanker but that is probably because he is posh and English. Most of the survival people on telly are posh and English like Ray Mears and Ed Stafford and most posh English people are wankers. But I had got a Bear Grylls knife off Amazon and it was brilliant, the same one he used, with a full tang.

'Don't call Bear a wanker Peppa' I said.

And she went 'Wanker' again and ran off down the slope.

I picked a run and followed it through more brown bracken, I kept looking back to the rock and approximately fifty metres down I came to a bit where there was just grass and it was that velvety thick bladed grass that is light green and the run went straight through the middle of it. Then I heard Peppa shout 'Rabbit!' and she was running back up to me chasing one. It smashed up through the ferns and into the clearing where I was with Peppa almost on it, but it turned sharp when it saw me. Peppa had the face on she always has when she runs, like she is biting her bottom lip and pushing her tongue out under her lip. When the rabbit swerved she tried to change direction and she was going so fast she toppled and rolled into the bracken and it cracked and hissed. 'Bastard' she said.

I said 'Run up to that tree and get some twigs' and she took off towards the oak. You need twigs to hold the snare open on the run and you have to set it a hand's width above the ground so it is in line with the rabbit's head. I got the first snare out and rubbed a bit of mud on it to mask the human smell but rabbits don't have a really keen sense of smell like rats or moles, they have good hearing and they communicate by thumping the ground to warn each other. They also have good eyesight so I wrapped long strands of grass around the shiny brass to make it more camouflaged.

Peppa ran back down with the twigs and I pushed them into the ground and set the snare open across the width of the run and then hammered in the peg with the butt of my knife. Peppa said 'Will that get one?' and I said 'Aye it will. We'll have to leave it overnight, but it will get one.'

And I believed it would because if you believe something will happen then it does, so you have to be careful about what you believe will happen. I believed that I would stop Robert and make Maw safe for nearly a year and then I did.

We set three more snares, one on the run we'd followed further down and then two more on another run that went parallel to the loch at the bottom. Then we went out wide of the area where I thought the rabbits were so we didn't scare them back down the slope to the loch.

Peppa said 'Let's go down to the loch' and she started running down through the ferns and trees towards the water. I tried to estimate how far I was from the loch in metres. I estimated it was seventy metres, and I knew my stride was ninety centimetres because I had measured it. So I worked out that if I took seventy-seven strides going straight down it was more or less seventy metres. (You divide 7,000 centimetres by 90 and that is approximately 77.7.) This is one of the things I learned to do, estimate distance, and I am good at maths and I know times tables and how to divide in my mind. So if I need to I can work out how far away something is or how long it will take to get to me and that is important for survival. I did seventy-seven strides straight down and got to the lochside and the little beach of flat stones and the water was about fifty centimetres from where I stopped so that wasn't bad.

The loch was long and turned a corner so from the beach you couldn't see the end like you could up on the slope. Trees came all the way down to the water all around except on the bit we were. There was a little beach and because of the angle of the slope behind me I estimated the depth to be about a metre and a half deep three metres out, but you can't really tell for sure because there could be holes or gullies in the rock under the water which would make it deeper. It was flat calm and still. The north breeze had dropped from the morning and the water was like a sheet of glass or highly polished steel. You could see it was yellowy brown in colour but clear quite far out because there had been no substantial rain in this area for close to three weeks. I had checked every day before we came.

Peppa was balancing about three metres out on a rock she had jumped to from some little stepping stones that went out from the beach.

'Don't get your trainers wet Peppa' I said.

'Alright. Hey Sal I can see fish here . . . wee stripey ones.'

She *could* actually get her trainers wet because they were made of Gore-Tex which is both waterproof and breathable but if water got in over the top we'd have to dry them out on the fire or they would be dangerous to wear for too long and cause athlete's foot and other fungal infections. We had to be careful about infections, I had told her this.

Even wee cuts and grazes, because I only had four Amoxicillin tablets which I found in the bathroom cabinet. In my first aid kit I had plasters, iodine, cotton wool, two bandages, safety pins, scissors, Savlon cream and some anti-depressants called Citalopram 30. I thought they might come in handy if Peppa got depressed like Maw. They never seemed to do Maw any good but that might be because she was drunk so much they probably didn't work. Like, you can't mix antibiotics with alcohol because the alcohol stops the antibiotics from killing bacteria which cause infections. But we didn't have any alcohol and we weren't going to get any, even for medicinal purposes.

I also had some paracetamol and ibuprofen and codeine, which is the best painkiller available without a prescription, in case we got hurt or got a sprain or a twisted ankle or I got my period and got period pain. We did periods in P6 and I am thirteen which is the age they said you mostly started getting them. I hadn't got it yet but planning for potential problems is an important part of survival. Also we could use sphagnum moss, which was everywhere, as an antiseptic on wounds like they did in the First World War.

The wee fish were perch. The loch is called something in Gaelic like Dubna Da and it contains pike, perch, brown trout and eels. We were going to fish for all of these with the rod and reel I nicked off Robert. He most likely nicked it anyway.

It was a ten-foot telescopic spinning rod with a screw reel seat and the reel was a fixed spool Shimano loaded with 10lb line. I had other fishing stuff too. Size 10 and 12 hooks, BB split shot, and some small trout spinners and lures in a plastic pack I nicked from the tackle shop. I also had two pike plugs and three wire traces, which you need for pike to stop them biting through the line.

Robert sometimes went down to the wall in the summer to spin for mackerel and he once brought three back and Maw shrieked and he didn't know how to gut them or cook them and he just stood there waving them about with Maw shrieking and going 'Fuck off with them Robert'.

So I watched a YouTube and then gutted and baked them with salt and me and Peppa ate them while Maw and Robert were at the Fishermen's. And they were lovely and tasted sweet.

The sun was fully up now and it was warm on us and Peppa skipped across the stones to the beach and unzipped her Helly Hansen and chucked it down on the rocks and then jumped up onto the grass and started pulling at it and overturning wee rocks and stones.

She is nearly as tall as me and she is only ten and her skin is the colour of dark honey and in the sun it looks gold. Her hair is frizzy and afro and ginger and she has freckles. I think she will be very, very beautiful when she is a woman. Her teeth are very white and she loves cleaning them and biting things with them. She bit Robert's hand once when he was hitting Maw and he backhanded her across the room and called her a wee cunt and I jumped on her to stop him hitting her again and he kicked me in the back twice and I had a bruise that went purple then yellow and I was off school again.

I was off school a lot and I worried they'd send the plunkieman to get me to go but they never. Our flat was on the second floor of Linlithgow House. There are three blocks all named after royal palaces on a hill above town and you can see the wall and the sea from the balcony. The other blocks round the court are Falkland and Scone. The entryphone lock was knackered in ours and you just shoved the bottom door with your shoulder. The hall was light blue and smelled of piss and junkies sometimes slept under the first set of concrete stairs going up.

Peppa stopped crying the same time as I did when she was about eight and we neither of us have cried since then. If she is angry she looks down and bites her bottom lip like she does when she is running and if she is sad I make a cradle with my arms and rock her.

She shouted 'Sal . . . worm!' and held up a lobworm she'd found. Lobworms are very good bait for perch and brown trout and are unusual in acid soils like the area we were surviving in. Peppa skipped back across the rocks and onto the big stone out in the loch and held the worm over the water. She called across to me 'See if he'll take it . . .' and she dangled the end of it into the water from her fingertips. I was just going to say there was no point without a hook when there was a swirl in the water and splash under the worm and Peppa shouted 'Bastard!' and looked over at me with her eyes wide and her mouth open. 'He took it! He was a big one Sal. Get another worm!'

For the first time since we came here I missed my phone. I wish I could've filmed her squatting in the sun on that rock in the flat glass water and beaming and looking happy. I decided to remember it there and then in my mind in case it didn't happen again. The sun was in her face and she called across 'Nice here innit?'

And I said 'Aye' and jumped up onto the grass and started pulling tussocks up to find a worm. It took ages and the one I found under a rock was flat and reddish and I don't know what species it was. I jumped out on the wee stones and jumped up next to her on the rock and now she was an expert and she took the worm and went on in a sing-song voice '. . . you just dangle it like this and let the wee fishy see his tail in the water . . .'

I said 'Was he spotty or stripey?'

She said 'Spotty. Gold and big red spots. What's that?'

'Brown trout' I said.

'Can ye eat it?'

'Aye. We can catch them with spinners too.'

'We should've brought the rod. Why does he eat spinners?'

'He doesn't eat them, he thinks they are prey.'

'But they're metal.'

'Aye, but they flash and look like wee fish when you spin them.'

She turned her head and stared at me. 'You know everything' she said.

'Aye, I do' I said.

But the big trout didn't come back so we dropped the worm in down the side of the rock and watched a wee Perch dart out and take it. This would be a good place for fishing and we would come back tomorrow with the rod.

We started back up the slope with the sun high above us. Peppa walked until we came up to the clearing in the bracken where the grass was greenest and thick and we'd set a snare. Two rabbits sprang out of the grass in front of us and tore off up towards the warren and Peppa took off after them. I watched her springing along through the fern with the rabbits, two brown blurs in front of her and their white arses flashing.

Then Peppa stopped dead and shouted back to me there was a rabbit in a snare we set. She went 'Sal. Sal lookit!' and I sprinted up into the clearing.

It was a big long one caught perfect round the throat and bucking and jerking against the cord and the peg. Peppa said 'I chased him in, I saw him go in it. There's blood!'

A dark ring of blood was emerging from the throat where the snare wire was clenched tight like a ball, the blood started spraying and flicking in drops on me as the rabbit bucked and I knelt down next to it. I have never killed anything apart from Robert but I was not bothered about it and this was going to be our first kill surviving and I'd seen it done loads of times on telly and YouTube. I grasped the rabbit round the throat and lifted it tugging the snare peg up. It was letting out a high scream like air hissing. I squeezed the neck and the snare ball and felt warm blood flood out onto my fingers. Then I got its back legs that were kicking and caught them in my other hand and pulled as hard as I could and felt a crack under my fingers round the throat and the rabbit hissed and went stiff and then flopped.

Peppa said 'Fuck me.'

And I said 'Don't swear.' I dropped the rabbit down on the grass and it jerked once when it hit the ground and then went still. It was a big buck. Plenty of meat and a great first snare for us. I felt brilliant.

Peppa stroked its fur. She said 'He's warm. Is it a boy or a girl?'

'Buck or a doe' I said.

'Aye. Buck or doe?'

'A buck. And he's gonna be our tea.'

'I chased him in didn't I not?'

'You did aye. You herded him like the Sioux with buffalo.'

'Did I? Tell me about them.'

'I'll tell you stuff later. Tonight when we go to bed.'

She said 'Okay.'

We walked back up the slope towards the thicker woods and the burn and I held the rabbit by his legs and he was heavy. Then I remembered you've got to de-pee them, so I held him by his head and ran my hand down his side and over his stomach and the pee came out from between his legs in a dribble.

· 17 ·

Chapter Two

Shots

That afternoon I made a barrier to go behind the fire and reflect heat back towards the shelter and Peppa practised with the slingshot after she had finished the belVitas. With a Bear Grylls knife you can either use the serrated sawing blade to cut wood or you can use a stone as a hammer and hit the blunt side of the blade into a branch at the bottom until it is mostly cut through and then rip it off. I used living branches from birch for the uprights and cut points into the end and then hammered them in with a stone until they were about a metre high. Then I wove branches in between, mostly smaller birch, some alder and some hazel sticks from a pollarded hazel by the burn. The barrier was curved and ran along the front of the shelter about two metres back from where we slept on a raised bed made from birch and alder poles and covered with spruce branches which made a very soft bed and they also insulate and they smell nice.

Peppa collected small round stones from the burn and used them as ammo to practise with the slingshot and I explained the principle of trajectory to her which is that as the speed of the projectile drops the force of gravity comes to bear on it and it falls at a given rate per metre that it is travelling with the fall rate directly related to the speed – so the slower it gets the faster it falls. If you can work out at what point in a given distance the projectile starts to drop then you can make a basic estimate of its eventual position in relation to the target. So that means you can adjust your firing position relative to the target so it is going at maximum speed when it hits it, or you can alter the angle of the aim up or down to make the projectile go in a rising then falling trajectory towards the target. This means you can stand further away and calculate the angle you need to hit the target, but the further away you stand the higher the aim angle needs to be and the less velocity the projectile will have when it hits the target.

So I told Peppa all this about the slingshot and trajectories and she looked at me and frowned and then said 'Righty-ho Sal' and started firing stones at the belVita box.

There is an optimum distance from target you can eventually find which ensures the necessary velocity for a kill, the least falling trajectory and the necessary distance from an animal or a bird so you don't scare it. I told Peppa to try and find that. I thought that if the stone punctured the cardboard of the belVita box then that was probably enough power to kill a rabbit or a pheasant or a grouse from whatever distance she was shooting from.

She said 'Could this kill a deer?'

And I said no because you'd never be able to get close enough to it for the stone to have the necessary power. Deer have hard skulls. Even if you went for a neck shot it would be unlikely to pierce it. I wondered if Robert's airgun would kill a deer. It would go through 9mm plywood on ten pumps at a distance of about twenty metres and I should think that would go through a roe deer's skull, and it would definitely go through the neck but I am not sure you could get that close to a deer unless you sat silent downwind for a long time. Most deer rifles are 30-06 or 30-30 calibre which is a very high speed bullet and maintains its power over very long distances like up to a kilometre. And it is a real bullet powered by a cartridge and explosives, but Robert's rifle is only a .22 airgun and the muzzle velocity is restricted by law. So you would have to get really close. But I thought I might try. A deer would provide meat for several days and they don't hibernate and I fancied getting camouflaged and stalking one.

Ed Stafford caught one, in some woods in Poland or somewhere like that he was surviving in, with a snare made from a bent-over sapling that triggered and strangled the deer. He skinned it and used the skin for a jumper and he buried the meat in a pit fire to cook it and he hung a load up over the fire so bears didn't get it. There are no bears in the Galloway forest so we didn't have to worry about that and I thought I might have a go at making that snare in a few days when we were properly settled in and we knew nobody was looking for us.

I collected more wood for the fire, I got dead branches mostly off trees or leaning up off the ground because they are the driest. I made a long pile the length of the shelter and stacked another pile next to it to dry and use later then I got birch bark for tinder and used the flint and steel to make a spark and blew it until I got a flame and fed in dry grass and twigs and got it going. I used burning twigs to start two more points at the end and in the middle so it would all burn along its whole length. Even after a few minutes I could feel the heat bouncing off the barrier when I sat on the raised bed.

Then I gutted the rabbit and although I had never done it before I had watched it done loads of times and it was easy and I kept the liver, heart and kidneys for fishing bait because they are good for eels. To skin a rabbit first you cut off the head and the paws, then you pull the skin down each leg until they pop out and then you drag the whole lot back up the body slowly until it all comes off in a oner.

Most of the meat on a rabbit is on the legs and the haunches and so I cut it in half and put some McDonald's salt on it and laid it on a big flat stone over the fire to cook. Then I went down to the burn and washed my hands because of infections and food poisoning.

I had seen a video of Inuit women in Alaska curing and stretching skins on round frames made from alder saplings, so I cut a long one and made a circular hoop about a metre diameter and bound it with paracord. Then I laid out the skin and made a series of little holes around its perimeter with the Bear Grylls knife. Then I threaded paracord through one, then over the frame, then back through the next one all the way round until the skin was stretched out across the whole frame.

When I was doing this sitting by the fire and with the sun starting to go down and the northerly breeze picking up and making my fingers cold, and the smell of the fire and it cracking and popping, I felt for a minute like I had always done this. I had always been able to thread a rabbit skin onto a frame and this wasn't the first time.

It felt funny, and I couldn't remember for a minute if I had ever done it or if I had only seen them doing it on YouTube. And for a minute, or for a few seconds really, I felt a bit dizzy and I could only see my hands threading the cord through the skin and over the hoop and back through the skin and back over the hoop and pulling it tighter. I couldn't feel the fire on my legs or the cold on my hands or hear the crackles or Peppa shooting at the belVita box, I could only see my hands and the thread and the little holes in the skin and the dark bark on the alder hoop and my hands moving like it wasn't me. Like I was a big eye watching it. And behind the big eye was a big black space and I was peering out from an eye-shaped hole in it at my hands threading the cord through the skin and over the hoop.

And then I came back and I was still threading the cord and the rabbit was starting to sizzle on the stone and Peppa came running over with the slingshot and belVita box and said 'I can hit it but it just dents it, look . . .' And she showed me the little dents and dinks in the yellow cardboard.

We turned the rabbit over and put more salt on it and it smelled lovely and was going brown and gold like toffee and hissing. The fire was getting really hot and Peppa laid out on the bed and took off her Helly Hansen and trainers and joggy bottoms and stretched out in her knickers and vest and went 'Aaah, lovely warm – these are prickly Sal', patting the pine branches.

The rabbit tasted good and it was all cooked through and Peppa ate most of it but I had a leg and a lot of meat from off the top along the spine they call the saddle. It is good to eat freshly killed and cooked meat because it contains small amounts of vitamin C which you need so you don't catch scurvy which makes your teeth fall out and you go mad. Old sailors and people on Arctic expeditions used to get it before they started eating lemons which have a lot of vitamin C in them, and so does kale and red peppers. But I also had multivitamins for us so we didn't get scurvy or other illnesses caused by vitamin deficiencies like osteoporosis, osteopenia and gout.

We boiled water from the burn in the kettle and had tea with McDonald's milk and sugar. We had a mug each, they were enamel and mine was blue and Peppa's was green.

I banked up the fire with new wood all along and Peppa jumped up and ran down behind the shelter to do a wee and a poo in the latrine I had dug with a stick on the first day we got here. She went barefoot and came hopping back going 'Oooh it's fucking cold . . .' The latrine was the first thing I made when we got to this site, it's about seven metres away from the shelter, down from it in case it rains but close enough so you can still see the fire glow from it. But it is black out there behind you when you are going and you have to face the shelter so you can see the fire and not think about the black behind you. You wipe your bum on grass. I had cut a big bunch of it and put it by the latrine on a flat rock where you can see it and it will dry a bit.

It was probably only about 6.30 but Peppa climbed into the double sleeping bag on the bed and I took my shoes off and took off my fleece and got in with her and she wriggled and went 'weeeeeeeecosy!' We had two blankets as well, one was a fleece blanket from IKEA and one was an old pink pure wool blanket with a satin edge I brought from the flat where it had been in the airing cupboard for years and nobody used it.

The rabbit skin on the frame was lying flat on the damp leaves with the skin down and the fur up. I didn't want it to dry out because tomorrow I was going to scrape all the bits of meat and fat off it and then cure it with wood ashes and wee and oak leaves, which have got tannin in them and they are meant to make the skin soft and supple. Inuit women chew the skin side and mash it all up with spit to stop it drying hard and snaggy. The chewing breaks down the skin tissue and I think spit must preserve it too because that is how they cure skins and furs. But you can make it soft with wee and ashes and oak leaves, where you make a paste and spread it on and let it soak in for a few days, and that preserves it according to a site I looked up about curing skins and furs. I didn't know if it would work or not.

Peppa went on the fire side and I went on the tarp side but I was really warm even though the wind was getting up again and swishing the last leaves on the birch trees, but it must've shifted from north because it wasn't coming in from the top like the night before. It was hitting the back of the tarp and making it billow in and out so it was probably a westerly or a northwesterly, but I didn't have my compass to check and I was starting to feel very sleepy.

Peppa said 'Tell me about the Sioux and the buffalo.' She likes me to tell her stuff every night and I like it too. Sometimes I have to make things up if I don't know all the correct facts and dates and places but I don't tell her because she thinks I know everything. And mostly I do. Especially about the Sioux and the buffalo and the Indian Wars of the 1860s in the Great Plains.

So I told her about how the Dakota Sioux migrated to the Great Plains in the eighteenth century and built a culture based on hunting the millions of buffalo that lived on the plains in herds so big a man could ride past one for a whole day and not see bare ground. And how the braves would ride alongside the herds and use their horses to split off small groups and drive them away across the plains towards a cliff edge where they would all run over and be killed in their hundreds on the rocks below. It was the most dangerous way of hunting the buffalo and that was why they did it because a brave could show his courage and skill on a horse, and one successful hunt in the autumn would provide food and shelter and clothing for the entire tribe for a whole winter and the winters in the Great Plains were savagely cold with feet of snow and freezing north winds.

And when I got to this bit Peppa was asleep and I kissed her ear and made a spoon behind her and listened to the wind and crackle of the fire with my eyes closed.

Chapter Three

Hooks

When I woke up I started to worry straight away that it was four days since we ran and this was the fourth day here and they would definitely be looking for us all over. I think it was our fourth day here. I think they would've found Maw in the room by now and she had a phone so she could phone out. But the room was locked from the outside and the key was on the carpet and there was no way she could've killed Robert and then locked herself in there from the outside so that proved she didn't do it.

And they would've found Robert on my bed and all the blood from his throat where I stabbed him three times. And blood up the wall too, on the wallpaper with monkeys on it. And Peppa gone too and her room just normal. They didn't know about the school uniforms we wore or the rucksack or the backpack Peppa carried or the hockey stick case with the gun and the rod in it, so if they looked for things missing they wouldn't know what was and wasn't there. I knew what was there and what we'd taken but the polis and social workers wouldn't know that. They'd find my T-shirt and jeans and knickers with Robert's blood all over them in the washing in the bathroom so they'd know it was me. They'd find the lock on Peppa's unlocked door and the key on the floor so they'd know I locked her in and it wasn't her.

I wondered if Maw had gone on telly asking us to come back and saying we weren't in any trouble. Or if they thought I had kidnapped Peppa. And they wouldn't find the knife because I had it with me. I got rid of all the phones I used to look stuff up and I dumped the laptop in a skip the day before I did it. I threw the phones off the wall into the sea where it is deep even at low tide and you go spinning for mackerel.

They would also find the phones Robert got and brought back and the cards he had and they knew him anyway because he had been in the jail once and he had a court appearance coming up in November for theft. They'd find bits of weed and speed and mandy all over the place and they'd know it was Robert's. And they had been to our flat twice two years ago, once when Robert was hitting Maw and me and once when Maw nicked two bottles of vodka from the Spar and got seen with them walking up to the flats and somebody shopped her.

If the polis were clever they'd trace the things I bought on the stolen cards over the eight months when I was planning it, but I'd put all those cards back in Robert's drawer or chucked them and most of them had been cancelled by the time I tried to use them. But if one copper was clever enough to look at purchases on stolen cards from Robert he'd see all the stuff I bought on Amazon like a tarp and a compass and the knife and mess tins and Peppa's trainers and the rucksack. And if he thought about it he might've had an idea what I was going to do. But coppers are not that clever and most of them I have met or seen on the telly are really thick and they don't arrest the people they should and they do arrest the people they shouldn't.

When they came round when Robert was hitting Maw the woman copper asked Maw if she was alright and Maw said aye and it was all just a rammy and shouting and no hitting. And the woman copper said to her 'Are you absolutely sure?' and Maw said 'Aye.' The man copper had taken Robert in the other room when she said this to Maw. And she didn't ask me anything but I wouldn't have told her anyway because they'd bring the social in and we'd get split up. Peppa was watching telly.

You could hear everything in our flats. A guy called Big Chris lived above us. He sometimes bought weed and mandy off Robert. At night you could hear him banging and screaming and crying. I don't know why. We nicked his broadband most of the time because Robert got his wifi code. Robert got phones and SIMs too, some of them could get 4G. I mostly went to McDonald's to get online when I was buying stuff with the cards. I used to get a McFlurry and sit facing the door so I could see who was coming in.

I got the school uniforms from a charity shop in August. They were two blazers and skirts and ties and blouses and mine was a bit tight but Peppa's fitted her and I paid ten pounds for them and told the wifey in the shop they were for a school play. They were from a posh school in Glasgow and had gold and red badges with 'Ad Vitam' embroidered on them and that means 'for life' in Latin.

We both wore our walking trainers with them and they looked alright and I carried the rucksack and the hockey stick case and Peppa carried the backpack. And we left the flat at 6.00 a.m. and nobody saw us, and we went through the close the back way and up the alley and climbed over the fence onto the path by the park that led along to the train station, so we didn't even walk on any roads or places where people would be and we got the 6.15 to Glasgow and I bought the tickets in the machine with the cash from Robert's wallet. I worried on the train and in Glasgow that we'd see kids who went to the posh school in real life and they'd know we didn't go to their school and they'd remember us. But we didn't.

In Glasgow where we changed trains it was crowded and there were hundreds of people all over rushing and walking and talking on phones and nobody even looked at us. When we got on the train to Girvan there was only one old wifey in the carriage and she smiled at Peppa and it was like she was going 'She looks so sweet'. I just wanted people to see two nice posh little girls going on a train to a posh school and they did.

Peppa asked if we had to talk posh if we talked, and I said no, don't talk till we get to the forest. Or if the police issued descriptions Maw would tell them what we would be wearing and then people would look for two girls wearing those things and not school uniforms like we were. If they saw us on CCTV we'd be two posh girls in school uniforms not two schemies from our flats and I told Peppa to look down all the time at the station so they didn't see our faces.

With the sleeping bag and the blankets and lures and spinners and the kettle stand and kettle the rucksack was heavy, but it was properly packed and had a waist strap so once it was on it was easy to walk with. Peppa carried most of the food in her backpack and also the first aid kit and spare paracord and the slingshot and some fishing stuff and airgun pellets.

At Girvan we went in a café by the station and Peppa had a big Scottish breakfast and I had bacon and egg and sausage and toast. The man in the café just said 'There you go girls' when he brought the food and that was all he said and we paid and went and then got the X22 to Newton Stewart which goes all along the edge of the Galloway forest park. I had to get the map and keep checking for our stop and I rang the bell when we were near it by a village called Glentrool. And the bus stopped and we got off and the driver didn't even look at us.

Then we walked up a little road towards the village and when we came to a green wooden sign that said 'Galloway Forest Park' we went into the car park and then walked along a path through some pine woods. We went into the woods and changed our clothes and buried the school uniforms and the two phones we had. I took the batteries and the SIMs out and put them in a bin in the car park because phone batteries have lithium in them which could leak out and cause pollution in the soil.

Then we climbed a bit and the path came round and out and we were looking down a valley towards Loch Trool and there were mountains with forest going up on either side and far away at the end on the other side was a bit that stuck out into the loch called the Bruce's Stone where Robert the Bruce lived and fought the English with a gang of men in 1307. He had lived wild in the hills and slept in caves and shelters.

It was all lit up with sunshine, and from the height of the sun and working out the times we'd been on the train and bus and walking I reckoned it was only about just before 11 o'clock in the morning.

And the night before I had killed Robert and locked Maw in her room.

I could feel the start of the glow of the sun through the trees but it was still dark and Peppa was fast asleep. It was really cold and there was frost on the burned ends of the sticks in the fire and the whole length of it was dusty ash but I could see some smoke coming from the middle where there were lumps like charcoal. The stone we cooked the rabbit on was split into three flat ovals that looked like roof slates, like we'd sliced it. I thought they'd make good plates.

We had two head torches and a solar charger but I was trying to get used to the dark and seeing and the more you sit in the dark the easier it gets to see. Even in pitch black you can sense things like animals do. And I am not scared of the dark and neither is Peppa. At night here it is so black and there is so little light pollution from towns and cars you can see the Milky Way and the stars give you a bit of light to see by even if there is no moon. It's only glow and not proper light and it starts to go down before the sun comes up and that is one way you can tell when dawn will be if the sky is clear.

The wind was picking up now and it was a cold one. I slid out of the sleeping bag and found my trainers and joggers and pulled them on. I zipped my fleece up and then blew the embers back to glowing and started a little fire with three half burned twigs. I crumbled some dry birch bark on and it fizzed and cracked and gave me more flame, then I started building a pyramid fire with ends of burned sticks and some of the sticks from the dry pile and waited for it all to take and a nice yellow flame to come out. The wind was catching the smoke and sending it straight away from me so the wind was a northwesterly and it was starting to blow.

I got the kettle and ran down to the burn to get water. In the SAS Survival Handbook it tells you to always filter water even if it comes from a running burn, but I read in other places that so long as you boil it, it's safe because boiling kills bacteria like Weil's disease which comes from infected rodent urine, and also kills parasites and flukes.

The burn was bubbling and rushing and there was a stone where you came out of the woods where you could kneel and fill the kettle in a fast-moving bit that ran over smooth rock and as I knelt to fill the kettle I looked up and there was a deer. There was enough light to make it out standing still as stone and staring straight at me from only about six metres away on the other bank. It was a young doe and I froze as still as it.

And we stayed like that. Paused like a DVD and staring, and I tried to become aware of my breathing so I didn't think and move and so I wouldn't feel the cold stone under my knees. And my breathing slowed so it was soon so slow I didn't know it. Then I felt a sensation like someone very gently tapping the top of my spine, slowly just tapping. And I saw things starting to drop down around the deer like little pricks of light, and they dropped with each slow tap. I stopped feeling the stones under my knees and hearing the burn bubble and the leaves moving. The air stopped going in and out of my lungs and I felt light and then not there and just looking out again at the deer and the lights that dropped in lines like rain coming down dead straight. The deer just moved out of my vision like someone leaving a picture. It moved slow and calm and made no noise.

Then the sun was up and a slice of it was pushing over the top of the mountain above the forest and I stood up and walked back to the shelter with the kettle full.

Peppa was awake and squatting by the fire and she was eating the Dundee cake and she said 'I want tea Sal.'

She fed sticks into the fire and I put the kettle on the

frame to boil and got the enamel cups and put teabags in them. We had loads of teabags.

I said 'We're not gonna hunt deer.'

And Peppa said 'Alright.' Then she said 'How long have we been here?'

And I thought for a minute and said 'I can't remember.' And I couldn't.

I knew it was days and nights but I couldn't remember how many and in my mind I went through all the last day cooking the rabbit and doing the skin on the hoop of alder and Peppa doing slingshot and snaring the rabbit and the big trout and the worm in Peppa's fingers and seeing the warren and Peppa calling Bear a wanker and coming down the slope in the sun and going through the wood and eating belVitas for breakfast and waking up and feeling Peppa to see if she was cold and then being asleep and then there was a day before and I might've built the shelter that day or I might have built it the day before that or before that and dug the latrine and the long walk over from Glentrool with the rucksack and sweating in the sun and I didn't know when that was or if it was yesterday.

Peppa said 'You alright Sal?'

I think I started to panic then because my breathing got fast and I felt butterflies in my chest. I only panic if I can't remember things I need to or if I don't know where I am or if we lose the map or the compass. When I tried to go into my memory for the days just past it felt like a big mush and I didn't get the pictures and things in order, I got a big rush and a mush. The number never just came into my head like it had.

Then I got the tapping on my spine again and started to see the little light pricks dropping slowly and I started to get more calm. And I tried to become aware of my breathing and felt calmer and the little lights dropped down in the wood behind Peppa's head and then I went warm and wanted to smile.

I said 'I couldn't remember.'

And Peppa said 'Never mind. It doesnae matter.'

And she was right, it didn't. I tried for things that did matter. And I got that the size 10 and 12 hooks and the split shot were zipped into the inner pocket of the top part of the rucksack with the wire traces and the plastic pack of spinners and I had the rabbit liver and heart and kidney on a stone for bait and the rod was 2.3 metres fully extended.

Further back I got the way to tie a blood knot for the hook onto the line and how to tie in the trace with a dropper to take three split shot to make a little ledger rig for bottom fishing, and I got taught all that by Ian Leckie, Mhari's papa, who had been in the army and been on the fishing boats and once took me and Mhari fishing off the wall and we got a cod and a saithe.

I said to Peppa 'Let's go fishing.'

At the loch the wind was up and there was a big ripple on the water. The fish would be down and not on top like yesterday. And the wind was cold and stratus cloud covered all the blue sky. Stratus cloud means rain or snow and with the wind hammering up the loch from the northwest it felt like it would be snow.

I showed Peppa how to cast a spinner and we got two trout and a small perch. Then she dug for worms and I tried ledgering the rabbit liver on a size 10 as far out as I could cast. But I didn't get a bite. We used the three worms Peppa found and we got another trout and a big perch with black stripes and a spikey dorsal fin like a sail.

But the wind was getting too strong and cold for us and it started to spit sleet and went dark. We went back to the shelter and had Dundee cake and belVitas and tea. And then we collected as much wood as we could and made a really big stack and I built a long fire again. Then I went over to the bracken and dug up a big bunch of bracken roots and cleaned and washed them in the burn. They were fat and long and pure white. You can eat them roasted and they contain carbohydrates but you can't eat too many because they can give you cancer but you have to eat a lot. The poison in bracken is called ptaquiloside and it is destroyed by heat.

The snow started as it was getting dark with the wind driving it into the back of the shelter and it made it all white and the tarp sagged a bit on top of the paracord.

I roasted the fish and the roots on a flat stone with salt on them all. We used the split stone for plates and the roasted roots tasted like chips and Peppa ate loads of them. The fish was nice but the perch skin was jaggy and you couldn't eat it but the flesh was white and sweet. Then we had tea with UHT milk and sugar.

It was lovely snuggling in the shelter in the sleeping bag with both blankets and watching the snow swirling in the fire light and hearing the wind.

Chapter Four

Snow

Sometimes when I was about nine and Peppa was six and Maw wasn't too bad with the drink she would tell us about our das. It was before Robert came and after a man called Eddie Bean who used to come and smoke weed with Maw and stay the night.

Maw was sixteen when I was born and my da was called Jimmy and he was blond and he supported Rangers and Maw went to school with him and she said she loved him and they got a flat together when I was in her belly. Then my da got killed in a car he was in with three other lads going into Glasgow and the other boys all survived, one was in a wheelchair and was called Pally and you sometimes saw him in his chair going in the Spar. My da got killed because he was in the front seat and he didn't have a seat belt on and they were all drunk.

Maw said she cried and cried and the council gave her a new flat — our flat in our block that has a balcony and you can see the firth and the wall and the lighthouse right out at the end of the wall and at night it flashes once every forty-five seconds.

Our flat had three bedrooms, a kitchen, a bathroom with a shower and a bath and a living room with a door out onto the balcony. I mostly had washing drying on the balcony.

She brought me back to that flat after I was born and for nearly two years she looked after me and she says she didn't drink or smoke weed and she was doing an apprenticeship at Cutz in the precinct learning to be a hairdresser.

Sometimes when she was out I got looked after by Mhari's papa, Ian Leckie, and her nanna who was called Pat, and they knew my mum because she had been in school with Mhari's mum and Mhari was born three months before me. Mhari's mum wasn't there and when I asked Maw where she was Maw made a face and said 'I cannae tell you darlin', but she got in a bad way is all I know.'

Mhari and me were babies together a lot and we had a playpen in her papa's house which was down by the wall and had a garden and a shed.

Maw said she met Peppa's da in a nightclub and he was a Nigerian student who was from the southeast of Nigeria and was from a tribe called the Igbo. He was tall and his skin was brown and Maw said he was gorgeous. He was learning to be an architect and he played football for the college and he could speak English and Igbo and four other Nigerian languages and also French and a bit of Arabic and Italian and he knew Latin. I think that is maybe why Peppa is clever and learned to read very quickly and she also likes words especially swearing and she reads books which I don't, except the SAS Survival Handbook.

Peppa's da's name was Kenneth and Maw said he liked her because she was curvy which means she had big tits and she liked him because he was a gentleman and had a lovely speaking voice. She said Peppa is like her da and I am like my da because I am tall and blond and I have got big eyes and a big mouth like him and I am getting muscles on my arms. Peppa's da was a Catholic and my da was a Protestant.

I think I remember Peppa's da from when I was only about three and I was on the balcony and he was with me and he lifted me up and he was laughing. He smelled of perfume and his hands were soft and he held me and we looked at the lighthouse.

There was about ten centimetres of snow in the morning and we got the fire going again and had tea and then went to check the snares and we'd got another rabbit. There were tracks in the snow, I found rabbit, red deer, fox and, I think, red squirrel under an oak tree, but I think squirrels hibernate, so it might've been a bird.

We collected more wood and then I had to look at the shelter because the snow had dragged the tarp down. I made the shelter the day we got here in the afternoon after we had walked five miles in the sun with all the gear. It was hard and we had to keep stopping and having drinks of water. I used the map and the compass to plot the route we took right up the side of Loch Trool on a forestry road opposite the other road where we saw some cars through the trees. It was easy on the forest road but when we got to the end of the loch we had to go up and ascend over 500 metres to the top of the ridge. There was a sheep path on the first bit up over grassy slopes with big rocks but it got steeper as we went higher and Peppa had to stop and so did I. We just did a bit at a time and took it slow, which is what they all say on the websites when you are climbing up.

The shelter was made by stringing paracord across between

two birch trees and then fixing the tarp with the Velcro flaps to it and pulling it back to the ground so it was at an angle of about sixty degrees which is the best angle for shedding water. Then I held it down at the back with rocks and used more rocks to make three plinths under it then cut poles of birch to make the bed. Peppa got spruce branches and we laid them all over the poles and we used a lot so they were thick and insulated. And they prickle a bit but once they are pressed down they are very soft and comfortable. You have to build the bed platform off the ground to stop heat loss. We did all this after the five miles with all the gear to the most remote part of the forest I could find on the map which also had access to water and was in the trees.

But after the weight of the snow the tarp had got all pulled and rucked at the bottom and the paracord had stretched and sagged, and the middle of the tarp was getting a V in it which would let in water if it rained. So I decided we needed to make a bender.

A bender is a type of shelter that is loads of saplings arched across each other to make a dome shape. There was a diagram of one in the handbook and it said it was a good shelter for longer-term use which is what we wanted. I would cover it with the tarp and then spruce branches to insulate it.

When I told Peppa we were going to make a bender she grinned and said 'Aye, we are going to make a bender because you are a bender!' and she giggled a lot.

She is always saying I am a lesbian, but I'm not and she is only joking but it is a bit homophobic, but it isn't because I am not gay. But when my hair is pulled back or I wear it under a hat I do look like a lad.

Some things make Peppa laugh so much she can't stand up and she has spasms and sometimes you think she is an epileptic. One thing that makes her laugh like that is the word 'houmous'. When we were wee and I used to steal her food I got her some houmous in a tub and she loved eating it with bread dipped in it and then she asked what it was called and I told her and she nearly pissed herself. She also laughs a lot at the word 'meconium' – which is the name of a baby's first poo when they are just born and it is full of very dangerous bacteria. The word 'bender' for a gay makes her laugh and so does the word 'menstruation' for having a period. She also likes swear words like 'wanker' and 'bollocks' and she loves the word 'jobby', especially if you call someone a jobby. At school she got in trouble for writing 'Mrs Gammon is a jobby' on sugar paper on a display when she was in P6.

If she sees fat people in town or in the precinct, she goes 'Quick – hide the pies!' and this makes me laugh too. And sometimes she goes 'Oooh . . . someone's found the key to the pie cupboard!' She also likes the word 'bumhole', and she sometimes says 'Stop being a drippy bumhole' if someone is annoying her or going on about stuff.

She likes Scots words as well like 'glaikit' which means that you are thick and your mouth is open and you look like you haven't got an idea in your head. And she also likes saying 'guy' for very and she likes the word 'dreich' for when it is damp and drizzling and dark, and if it is she'll go 'It's guy dreich the day.'

There was a kid in her class with a really big head called Robert McCulloch and she started calling him 'Heid' which is Scots for head. And soon all the other kids in the class were calling him 'Heid McCulloch' and he liked it because he had a nickname but Mrs Gammon said it was bullying and Peppa said 'Aye, but it is a guy big heid Mrs Gammon.'

She did Burns in school and learned the Mouse poem

and she sometimes says them and the bit that is best is '. . . still, thou art blest, compar'd wi' me! the present only toucheth thee: but Och! I backward cast my e'e on prospects drear! An' forward tho' I canna see I guess an' fear!' which he says to the mouse in the nest he's ploughed up and that is true and that is how I was in the flat and how I was for all my life and I want to be more like the mouse. Peppa calls women 'hen' like wifies in shops and if Maw was drunk she said she was 'unco fou'.

Another good thing about a bender is that we could keep it warm with just a pyramid fire instead of a long fire and that would use less wood and that was another good reason so I cut the tarp down and shook it off and then went to look for saplings and thinner branches and Peppa went and got wood to keep the fire going.

I lashed some of the saplings together thin end to thin end and made them about four metres long and sharpened the ends and then forced them into the leafy ground and that was not all that easy because there are a lot of rocks and stones in the ground, so I put little piles of stones around each one when it was in to hold it. I spaced the poles about two metres apart each and then looped them over and made a dome shape. It was not as easy as it looks in the handbook either.

The sun was out now and some of the snow was getting soft and dripping from the trees, and I was kicking snow and leaves and muck out from round the bed under the new dome frame when I heard the helicopter.

It was low and chugging and I knew what it was as soon as I heard it. I think I had been expecting it. And I shouted in a big whisper 'Peppa get down.' She was dragging some wood back towards me and she just dropped and rolled under a holly bush and I crouched. I was looking up through the dome frame and above me I saw it as the noise came louder going chop chop chop chop chop. It was white underneath with E90 RESCUE in black letters. It was so low I could've hit it with the airgun probably less than thirty metres. It went right over us under the trees crouching. Then it flew still low out towards the loch.

I stayed still and shout-whispered to Peppa 'Stay there.' Then I sprinted down towards the burn and jumped over the rocks and up the first slope into the trees. The noise was fading and when I came out in the bracken it was halfway down the loch, still low. Then Peppa was there beside me in the ferns and she got hold of my hand and said 'Is it after us?'

I said 'I don't know. I think it's mountain rescue.' It had disappeared behind the trees on the other side. Then we started to hear it again and it came out far over on the other side of the loch zooming along against the snow on the trees. It was coming back round and I grabbed Peppa and we rolled into the bracken and I pulled it closed on us and we lay there. The chop chop chop chop chop getting louder. And louder. And it must've come right back over us skirting our wood and heading north towards Magna Bra and the moor. The chopping faded. It was cold and damp in the ferns there on the snow and leaves, but I made us stay there and counted to 180 saying elephant in between each number to make it three minutes.

I said 'Let's go back.'

Peppa said 'Have we gotta move now?'

I said 'No. Not now. If it's mountain rescue it means they're looking for someone up there. In the snow.'

That meant there were people up at Magna Bra or on the moors above our wood.

I said 'Come on.' And we sprinted back through to the

shelter and I got the map and we sat under the dome frame and looked at it. Magna Bra was at the top of the moor above us and our woods stopped about a mile from the start of the moor.

'Ah'm going to look' I said and pulled the compass out of the rucksack.

'Ah'm coming' Peppa said.

'NO Peppa stay here and wait for me, they're looking for two of us.'

She said 'Nah' and got up and started sprinting north through the wood. I shouted but she was gone faster than I could get after her so I started off.

The burn ran north and you followed it all the way to the top of our woods. I was cracking through the sticks and bracken and trees but I couldn't see Peppa not even her back. It was all rising ground and the snow was thicker the further you went up. As long as we stayed in the woods we couldn't be seen from the helicopter or anyone out up on the moor, the trees broke up the outline and against the snow looking in you wouldn't stand out plus my fleece was grey and Peppa's was black and they are good camouflage colours. But not against snow in the open once we got to the top.

Following the burn up you could feel the trees start to thin out and see the moor rising up and I slowed down and started to creep and I was puffing from running and getting panicky about Peppa because I still couldn't see her. The sharp wind had started again and was blowing straight into me and stratus clouds were moving in from the north and I kept checking the compass. The wind was whooshing in my ears and I was stooping and running trying to stay low.

Finally the trees stopped and the burn went on into a gorge with steep sides and there was a ridge above me and I could see Peppa lying flat at the top and looking over it.

I wished it would get dark so we'd be covered unless they used a light. I could hear the chop chop chop far off again now as I ran up towards Peppa and she was peeking over the ridge top by a rock.

I got to her and jumped down next to her and peeked over. The moor was huge and white with ridges of snow and it rose up and there was a hill at the end and above that another hill. About 150 metres away the helicopter had landed but the rotors were still going and there were little flashes of orange and yellow from men's coats moving by it and snow was starting to come down again.

We watched through the snow and they were putting a stretcher in and there was three guys, two in bright-coloured coats and a guy in a blue thing and it looked like they had another guy on the stretcher.

Peppa said 'Wanky walkers.'

I said 'We need to get back in the woods before they take off.'

And we backed down the slope and ran back into the woods and got in far enough to be covered. We could hear the helicopter blades getting fast and watched it rise up above the ridge. They couldn't see us and the snow was starting to really blow in.

Peppa said 'You know what I fancy?'

I said 'What?' and she said 'Sausages.'

We didn't have any but we had a rabbit and we had to finish the bender so we walked back down the burn into the woods.

We had to work fast to finish the bender and stretch the tarp over it, and I made a doorway with an arch-shaped pole and bound it on with paracord, then we thatched it with spruce really thick and we put new spruce on the bed because it had got wet.

It started to get dark and the snow kept on but not as bad here as up on the moor and we got a pyramid fire going just outside the door of the bender and cooked the rabbit. We had tea and Peppa ate the last bit of Dundee cake. The bender was getting covered in snow and inside it felt warm because snow insulates.

They were the first people we'd seen since the bus driver on the day we came here. And although I tried not to I started to worry about it and them being there and there being walkers and wankers in cagoules up towards Magna Bra but they hadn't seen us and they hadn't been looking for us.

Chapter Five

Birds

The next day I made another hoop and scraped the new rabbit skin and then I used wood ash and oak leaves and wee to make the paste and I spread it over both of the skins and left them caked on the skin side to cure for the day. Then I washed my hands in the burn.

For food we had two boxes of belVitas, a cherry cake, a bag of brioches, two bags of walnuts and two bags of almonds and a big bag of raisins left. We needed to hunt again today for our main food and I decided to try to shoot birds with the air rifle.

There are a number of species of birds in the forest and on the moors. For birds of prey there are red kite, kestrel, sparrowhawk and osprey but osprey are migratory and would be gone by now. There are also golden eagles and white-tailed eagles and I want to see one of those. There are also owls, probably tawny owls. Other migratory birds you get here are great grey shrike and woodlarks.

The birds you can eat are black grouse and there are also capercaillie. Rich people come up here in August and shoot the grouse on the moor tops and I wondered if I could get one even though we only had an airgun and not a shotgun. I thought they would be easy to see with snow on the ground further up.

You needed a jumper because the wind was still northerly and although there hadn't been much more snow in the night it was cold and it cut you. It is wind that can kill you in the open, not cold, because wind chills and reduces temperature by convection so you need a windproof layer of clothing or a shelter to stop it. The best fabric is Gore-Tex, which is what Peppa's Helly Hansen is made out of. Gore-Tex stops wind but is breathable so it allows moisture from the body to pass through it in one direction only and you don't get a moisture build-up on the inside of your layers, which could freeze in very cold conditions and that would also kill you, eventually. Our fleeces were windproof too and I put on another sweatshirt over my T-shirt and checked shirt and then my fleece and Peppa had a purple lambswool jumper she put on under her fleece which creates layers to trap air and keeps you warmer. Soon I could make her a hat out of rabbit skin but I gave her my beanie and she already had gloves.

We went towards the burn, me with the airgun and Peppa brought the slingshot. I took the backpack with the pellets and belVitas and raisins and the map and compass and two waterproofs in case of precipitation and I had worked out a route that went along the top of the valley where the loch was and up and over, then skirted most of the moor round Magna Bra. It was four miles and would bring us back to our wood at the top. It was mostly along the edge of woods and bits of forestry planting and some bits were in the open on the moor. It was four miles and I thought it would take us all day because we were going to walk and not run. Also the first long bit along the valley was south facing so there would be less snow which had come in from the north. We were also going to stop and try to shoot birds if we could.

There was still stratus and still a north wind but it was less and more of a breeze. After we crossed the burn and went through the woods we found a deer path in the snow that led all along the valley top. It looked like there was a small herd of red deer and they might've been females and the path was recent and there were droppings and we just followed it. I kept scanning all around and listening and Peppa walked in front of me. If we saw anyone or heard a helicopter or a car or a ranger's truck we were going to drop and get straight into the forest, so we kept close to it, just on our right. And the deer had done the same thing. They don't like being too far away from cover.

Sparrowhawks fly low and fast along the ground and hunt in woods and they eat songbirds. Red kites fly high and circle and sometimes they circle carrion, like vultures in Africa, because that is mostly what they eat but they do hunt rabbits and voles and rats. Golden eagles fly high too but they can see prey from almost two miles away and when they start to descend to make a kill they go almost as fast as a peregrine falcon which is the fastest living creature on planet Earth. They like to roost in high places like trees and rocky crags and sometimes on fence posts at the top of moors and in winter they eat mostly carrion, like kites.

Most of the stuff I know, I know from Wikipedia and websites about things I am interested in, and also from YouTube videos and from TV. At school I was in a special unit for vulnerable learners where I could be online most of the day and I had to talk to Mrs Finlayson about my feelings.

I know a lot about survival, making fires and shelters, snaring food, making bird traps, filtering water, reading tracks and watching the weather. I also know a lot about British animals and most birds except sea birds. And fish and amphibians and reptiles. I know about trees and quite a lot of plants, especially if they are plants you can eat. I know the Latin names of all the native British trees. I also know about cooking and food hygiene and quite a lot about health and common ailments and alcoholism which is a disease. I know how to nick stuff and how to read timetables and how to set up email accounts which you need if you are buying stuff on Amazon with dodgy cards. I also know how to use a drill and fit locks in doors.

I can clean and hoover and make a healthy meal plan. I also know about some bits of history like the Indian Wars of the 1860s in the USA, the French Revolution, the Covenanters in the seventeenth century in Scotland and the Battle of Stalingrad in the winter of 1943. I am good at doing maths in my head and I know all the times tables so I can also divide and do fractions and percentages. I can shoot with an airgun and cast a fishing rod, but not a fly rod which uses a weighted line to get the fly out to the fish and I have never done that. I can read a map, do grid references, plot a course with a compass and work out elevations and gradients. I have killed one person, quite a lot of fish and, so far, two rabbits.

The hardest thing about killing Robert was not doing it or telling Peppa I was going to do it, it was telling Peppa what Robert had been doing to me and how he said he was going to start doing it to her. When I told her she said 'Kill him Sal' and I said 'Aye.'

She was worried about Maw but I told her the plan to lock her in her room so she wouldn't get the blame and then to run and survive. And she said she'd only do it if we went back and got Maw after a year so I said okay we would. She was pleased she wouldn't have to go to school and she knew that if anyone found out about Robert we'd get took and split up. Two boys in her class were fostered and they were brothers and they had a sister who was fostered in Edinburgh and they only saw her in a family centre once a month. And she said fuck that.

I didn't want to tell Peppa about what Robert had done since I was ten because she thought I was the best and cleverest and most brave person in the world and she thought I knew everything and I looked after her all the time and kept her safe. And if she knew about Robert I thought it would make me look soft and I should've bitten his cock off. When it started I was more amazed than scared and the way he spoke and the smell of drink and weed off him and his half closed eyes kept coming back into my head for days afterwards. So did what he said about telling.

Robert was skinny and he had a little fluffy beard on his chin and he smelled sour like vinegar or he smelled of drink. He had tattoos on both his forearms and a tattoo of a panther on his chest and roses and knives on his shoulder. He had veins that stood out on his arms and on the side of his head near his temple and his skin was grey and rough. Maw met him when she was lap dancing in a club in Glasgow when I was nine and Peppa was six and she had lost her job at Cutz for not coming in but she could still cut hair. And she said she wanted to be a dancer and she could dance and she had brown hair and big tits and she was pretty. Robert was a guy who dealt weed and pills to the girls at the club and he also got stolen cards and could sometimes get ones that got you cash from machines.

One morning there was four hundred pounds in twenties on the kitchen drainer and I took four of them for food and a new backpack for Peppa for school. That was the day

Robert first stayed and Maw said 'This is Robert Sal, he's my new boyfriend.' And I stare at people, not because I don't like them or because I am rude but because I need to get a really good look at them so I know. I stared at Robert and he said 'Geeza smile Sally' and Maw went 'Smile Sal' and I smiled with my mouth but not my eyes and he said 'That's better Blondie. I knew your da' and Maw said 'He did aye Sal, he knew Jimmy' and Robert said 'Sally Broon. Sally Broon.'

I could've told him my name is not Sally it is Salmarina which means sea salt in Spanish and Maw thought it up when she was sixteen and she thought it sounded classy and like a kind of wine. Peppa's real name is Paula but when she was wee Maw used to call her Wee Red Pepper because of her hair and then we all started calling her Peppa with an a. And then Maw said we were Salt-N-Pepa who are girl rappers from ages ago, because of my name and Peppa's new name, and we watched some of their videos like Shake Your Thang and Push It. I think the words are about sex but Peppa used to love them and stick out her arse and shake it about like they did on the videos.

Peppa was called Paula after a saint and a pope because her da was a Catholic. Robert started calling her Black Peppa because she was half African which is racist and it used to make Peppa go mad at him. He always was racist to her and called her half-breed and half-a-darkie, and she called him a fucking twat.

We have both got Maw's surname: Brown. Although my da's surname was Mazur because his papa's papa was Polish and he came to Scotland in the Second World War to build coastal defences. And Peppa's surname should be Adichie if she took her dad's name which she might one day. Maw's first name is Claire but when she was dancing she said her name was Nicole and sometimes she told people her name was Jordan.

They didn't notice the four twenties I took and after that whenever Robert was there I noticed where he put his money or his wallet and I robbed him when he was out of it. Soon he moved in, one day he came up with a holdall and his airgun and fishing rod and some golf clubs. I was in the flat on my own and Peppa was doing gymnastics at the centre and I was going to get her. I heard the key in the door and thought it was Maw and then Robert came in lugging his holdall and he said 'Ah'm going to stay for a bit alright?' and I said 'Does Maw know?' and he said 'Aye. She gave me the key. She got an afternoon shift at the club.'

Then he said 'Do you want to make us a cup a tea?'

And I said 'No.'

And he said 'Oooh alright. Are we going to be pals?'

And I said 'No.'

Then he said 'You're tall aren't ye?'

And I said 'Aye.'

And then he said 'Do you want a spliff?'

I said no and I had to go and get Peppa and he started making a joint in the front room on the sofa.

We stayed skirting the trees on the edge of the moor and followed the deer path all along but we saw nothing we could shoot. Then we came to a gorge where another burn came down into the valley. There was a little waterfall there and it plunged down into a pool with rowan trees and hazels and small oaks around it. The water thundered and you could hear it as you got nearer. As we got to the pool a huge heron flew up and its wings went slow. Peppa shot a stone at it and it swerved in the air and carried on flapping down into the valley. We climbed up alongside the gorge and came out at the moor where it goes up and up and the snow was sparkling and there was dry grass sticking out of it and blowing in the wind. The sun was breaking the clouds up and they were skidding along on the wind and when the sun came out there was a bright glare like headlights in your face off the snow. The show was crunchy and had a thin layer of ice on the top and was about fifteen centimetres deep. Peppa was squinting into the glare and the whiteness of the bank we were climbing made me feel dizzy and all you could hear was our feet crunching the snow. At the top there were big rocks and we sat with our back to them and ate belVitas and raisins.

We were looking out right across the valley across the loch, and you could see all the different woods, some were plantations in blocks and we could see the forestry track going along the top on the other side and in and out of them. Then I heard Peppa whisper 'Sal . . .'

She was lying on the snow looking up past the rock we'd been leaning on and she pointed. Further up in amongst little boulders were two grouse. They were both females and had grey and brown feathers with little black flecks and they were pecking at heather where it had got no snow on it at the sides of the boulders.

I tried to move as slow as I could as I got the airgun up and lay flat by the rock. It was pumped seven times and had a pellet in the breech. The grouse were close enough to hit and the nearest one had its back to me and I got the bead on the site on the middle of its neck. You have to squeeze the trigger and hold your breath as you get your finger round it and then release the breath slowly as you squeeze.

When I shot and the gun went *fut* both of them took

off and made a noise like 'tek tek' but the one I shot flew forward and then smashed down on the snow and rolled over and over and then started running and flapping one wing out. I said 'Peppa get it' and she got up and ran towards it, and I followed. The grouse ran along changing directions and going tek tek and there was a line of blood on the snow behind it. And it kept going with Peppa racing behind it and her feet stamping holes in the snow and me racing behind her holding the gun. The grouse was zigzagging all the time and Peppa kept slipping and stumbling. I was pumping the airgun to try to get another shot at it while it couldn't fly. One wing was trailing along the snow and the other was waving out and the blood trail on the snow followed it. Then it changed direction again and jumped and half took off and then crashed down again and rolled over and lay still.

It still had its eyes open when I got to it and it was breathing fast and the blood on the snow around it looked black. I put another pellet in the breech and shot it straight in the head point blank so it didn't suffer and its head thudded against the snow and more blood came out of the back of it. It was soft and warm and felt small and light when I picked it up and its head hung down. Peppa stroked it and said 'It's nice isn't it?' I said 'Aye.' Its feet were big and there were short claws and it had scales like a reptile because birds evolved from reptiles.

Peppa said 'Do you feel bad about it?'

And I said 'Aye,' and I did, even though we were going to eat it. It was small and soft when you held it and its beak was small and it had an orange bit over its eye that looked like eye shadow and it was pretty. We put the grouse in the backpack and carried on along and up onto the moor.

Chapter Six

Town

There wasn't much meat on the grouse and I let Peppa have most of it, but it was good with salt on it roasted on the stones. We walked the whole moor right up to another hill and then back round skirting right round Magna Bra. We didn't get any more birds but we saw kites and geese flying over. We didn't see anyone or any forestry 4x4s or helicopters. It was over four miles by the time we got back and collected wood and cooked the grouse.

That night I told Peppa about the Covenanters in Scotland who didn't want the English king's religion or bishops in the church and who had meetings out in the moors and hills in Ayrshire and Galloway at night. They had preachers who wore masks and talked about God at secret meetings, and from 1680 until 1688 there was a time called the Killing Time when the king sent soldiers down into this area and they massacred the Covenanters and made thousands of them go to Ireland. There was a woman called Margaret Wilson who wouldn't give up her religion so they got her and some others and tied them to posts in the Solway Firth at low tide. They gave her the chance to say she loved the king and would go to his church but she wouldn't so they let the tide come in over her and she drowned. And Peppa said 'Why didn't she just say what they wanted?' and I said 'I dunno,' and I didn't.

I would've. It doesn't matter what church you go to. We never went to church but we did some religion in school and a minister came in at Easter and Christmas and went on about Jesus. Even Peppa said she would've just told them what they wanted, and her da's a Catholic.

I found out about the Covenanters on Wikipedia when I was reading about Galloway and I saw the words 'The Killing Time' and googled them and there were things about Margaret Wilson and all the killing in Galloway then.

Next day we washed our knickers and socks and T-shirts in the burn and I made a clothes line out of saplings and paracord over the fire. I told Peppa we had to wash or we'd get dirty and you can get body lice and infections. And Peppa said 'Aye you're right hen, ah dinnae want a fishy fanny' and I said 'Me neither.'

We got the fire going and built right up and then I boiled the kettle and soaked our towel with hot water and Peppa stripped off and washed herself all over and kept shivering and jumping and going 'Aaah!' when I was rinsing and wringing the towel for her. She got a dry T-shirt on and hopped about by the fire till she was warm and dry and then got dressed. Then we boiled the kettle again and I stripped off. Peppa sat on a log watching me. The fire kept your front warm but your back and arse froze in the breeze which was still northerly.

Peppa said 'You're getting pubes.'

I said 'Aye.'

She said 'I don't want them.'

'Well, you'll get them.'

She said 'Will mine be ginger?'

And then I laughed. Sometimes she can make me laugh like that, like exploding and not knowing where it came from. And she was raging I was laughing.

'It's alright for you. I'm gonna have ginger pubes and they'll call me Ginger Pubes.'

'Who will?'

'Lads and that.'

'They'll not. They won't see them.'

'Aye, but they'll know. Because of ma hair.'

'Peppa you're gonna be beautiful' I said.

She was pushing her chest together trying to make a cleavage. She went 'Will I have tits like Maw with a cleav-erage?'

I said 'I dunno. I haven't.'

'Aye, but you're still growing yours Sal.'

Mine were tiny like pimples and I didn't wear a bra, I didn't need one. I didn't want big ones like Maw. Robert was always staring at them and grabbing them. I hadn't had a period yet either but I thought I might sometimes when my belly got sore and swelled up but I didn't. I knew what to do if I got it and I had some Always Ultra in the ruck-sack and some non-perfumed wipes. I also had the ibuprofen and codeine for period pain.

There were no rabbits in the snares so we took them up and we walked over from the first warren and found another one beyond the ferns and oak trees nearer the lochside and we set three more snares and left them. We went back to the bender and got more wood. The standing dry wood near us was all used up now and we were having to drag it back from by the burn or further up in our wood. I cut some more spruce branches for the top of the bender and for the bottom where the tarp didn't meet the ground.

We had no meat or fish that night and we ate cherry cake and walnuts and raisins.

The wind changed, the northerly dropped and it came from the west and it was warmer, and as we lay in the bender looking at the fire we heard hisses and splashes and trickles of rain coming down hard. It was melting the snow and wet blobs of it were dropping off the tree branches, and after an hour or so the fire was almost out and soaked and we could hear the burn rushing and churning with all the new water. I had stacked some wood in the bender to dry and I was glad. The bender didn't let any rain in and we fell asleep listening to it drumming down on us.

Next morning I got a little fire going right in the entrance of the bender and boiled the kettle and while I was waiting for it to get light I started worrying about the food. I still found it hard to work out how many days we'd been here or what day of the week it was. I thought if it was a Wednesday when we ran, that would make it a Sunday when we saw the helicopter if that was five days after we ran, but I couldn't remember what we'd done every day or how many nights I'd fallen asleep telling Peppa stuff. We'd had two rabbits because we had two skins and we'd had fish on two days and a grouse on one day. If I thought hard and counted I worked out it could be a Wednesday or a Thursday today.

We were short of food, and if we didn't snare a rabbit or get fish again we'd have to eat the last raisins and the brioches and then we'd go hungry. I could go hungry but Peppa couldn't, and I wouldn't let her and I was trying to work out how much food we brought to see us through to when we could hunt and snare everything. And I didn't want to, but I was thinking we maybe couldn't just eat what we caught or snared or dug up and that we needed more food.

It would take me a whole day to get into the town and

get food for another week and I'd have to leave Peppa here because they were looking for two of us and by now they had descriptions and maybe even CCTV from the train station and they maybe even knew we used disguises. I had a hundred and five pounds in the rucksack left from the money we brought. The thought of leaving Peppa made me start to feel a panic.

Peppa called out from the bed 'Any tea Sal?'

And I said aye, and made her some with a teabag and UHT and sugar. I gave her three of the brioches for her breakfast and she ate them in the bed as the sun was starting to come up. The rain was easing off but the wind was still blowing in from the west and it was warm and damp.

She said 'Snow's gone Sal. All the washing's wet.'

It was, still on the line I made and all dripping.

I said 'I think I'm going to have to go and get more food Peppa. And you can't come or we'll get caught. It'll take me all day and you have to stay here and stay in the bender.'

She thought for a bit then said 'Will you get me a book?'

I said aye, and she said 'Can I have the knife and the gun?'

I said aye, I'd pump the gun and put a pellet in it but she wasn't to shoot it unless it was an emergency and someone was attacking her. She said 'I'll be scared Sal.' And I said I know and I went over and hugged her and whispered 'You stay in the bender and don't go out. You'll be alright and I'll be back before it's dark.'

She said 'What if I need a wee?'

'Aye, well, you can go to the latrine but then come straight back in here and get in the bed and stay warm and wait for me.'

She said 'Can I cut up the rabbit skins and make a hat? I can sew it.'

So I said aye, even though I thought she'd make a mess of it. And I told her to be careful with the knife and always cut away from her and do it on a stone in the bender. I got her the sewing kit with extra strong thread in it and I threaded her a big needle. I got the rabbit skins off the frames and brushed all the ash and wee and oakleaf off them and scrunched them up and rubbed them to try to get them soft. I gave her the knife and told her to keep it in the sheath when she wasn't cutting with it because the sheath had a sharpener on the inside.

I left her the brioches and boiled water in the kettle and made her put on her purple jumper and her fleece. She'd been on her own in the flat before, when I was out getting things and Maw and Robert were in the pub or out in town, but she always had the telly then.

I took the backpack and the map and compass and the money. I left her in the bender cutting at the rabbit skins. I didn't say goodbye or make a big thing of going, I just turned and went. For the first mile through the forest I breathed steady and looked straight ahead and listened to my feet stamping on the leaves and twigs and brown larch needles.

I was wearing my fleece and had the backpack and a hat with my hair up in it and I thought I'd look like a lad out hiking because I had walking trainers and waterproof over-trousers on too. If someone saw me they'd think I was just a lad or a scout out in the forest.

I went along through the forest and then crossed onto a moor bit with heather and went along the edge of a plantation until it came out at the bottom of a hill, and over the hill was the next valley and then along the top of that was a slope going down to a forestry track that went along through more plantation spruce.

So I didn't panic about Peppa, I thought about Ian Leckie.

He was Mhari's papa and he looked after us when we were wee and he loved me. He was the only person who didn't think I was weird and didn't say 'What ye starin' at?' He was old and they lived by the shore in a proper house with a garden and a shed. Even after I stopped going about with Mhari I used to go there and see him and he called me Bonny Sal. Ian Leckie taught me about fishing and tying knots and he took me and Mhari to the wall and we caught a cod and a saithe on mackerel strip. He showed me how to gut mackerel and he thought it was funny I liked doing it and said 'There's no many lassies'll do that Sal.'

In his shed he had tools and paint cans and varnish and he made a hutch for Mhari's rabbit. He told me about plywood and how it is so strong because they glue crossing grains in thin sheets and compress them. He taught me how to saw a bit of wood and keep your elbow in so you don't go off the line you are cutting and he told me about how they use copper strips to stop barnacles and weeds growing on the bottom of fishing boats because they create an electrical current that stops them growing.

When I was sad about Maw or scared about Robert or going to panic I thought about Ian Leckie, and it made me feel calm and warm and I think I might have loved him like he was my papa. Ian Leckie didn't drink and he said he'd been sober twenty-two years but before that he was on the drink all day and night and he got arrested for fighting. He used to go to meetings to stay sober and not drink with other people who didn't drink at the Fishermen's Hall.

Once he met me and Maw and Peppa walking up from the precinct and Peppa was in a buggy and Maw had three bottles of cider in a carrier. He said 'Hello Claire, how you doing luv?' and Maw said alright and she seemed like she wanted to keep going but Ian Leckie put his hand on her shoulder and said 'Are you doing alright ma luv?' and Maw said aye and she was just wanting to get home and get the tea.

Ian Leckie rubbed my head and said 'How's ma Bonny Sal?' and then he squatted down and put his hand on Peppa's cheek and said 'Look at wee Peppa, what a bonny lassie.' And she smiled at him and she had no front teeth and he clapped his hands and made his cheeks go all blown up at her and she giggled.

Maw said 'See you Ian, come on Sal.'

And Ian Leckie said 'Ah'm going up the wall on Saturday for cod if Sal wants to come. She's a good gutter.'

Maw said 'Oh Ian we're out Saturday, awa' to Glasgow to see ma friend Jo. Come on Sal . . .' And she started back off up towards the flats. I knew we weren't out Saturday and I knew she didn't have a friend called Jo in Glasgow. My maw was a good liar. We got home and she started on the cider and me and Peppa watched telly.

After that when I saw Ian Leckie or I went down to his house to go in his shed he said 'How's yer maw?' and I'd say alright. And then he'd say 'Is she still on the drink?' and I'd say aye. And he'd say 'Tell her to come and see me if she needs a hand.'

But I didn't. She only really got angry and screaming if she had no drink or if I hid it and she found it or if I said to her not to drink it. She was alright when she got drunk and then for a while she was soppy and wanted to cuddle us. And then sometimes she'd cry and start phoning people on her phone and I'd get Peppa's tea and put her to bed. If I went back through she was normally asleep and you couldn't wake her, so I'd make sure her fag was out and cover her in a sleeping bag and go to bed or go online and read.

Maw used to take us thieving drink with Peppa in a

buggy. She could only get wine or cans like cider and extra strong lager because vodka and whisky have got tags on them and they set off the alarm when you go out of ASDA. Maw used to make me watch along the aisle and spot the CCTV and then she put the cans in under Peppa or in the wee tray under the buggy and piled coats on them. She used to bring extra ones for that. Once she zipped two bottles of wine into my coat and I had to hold my hand up on my chest when we went through the checkout. She said to be quiet and not to cry and to stand close to her when we went through.

I asked her if me and Peppa would get arrested too, if she got arrested, and she said 'No. But they'll take youse off me.'

I got to the end of the forestry road and then came out in the car park near where we buried our mobiles on the way here, then followed the path along onto the road and up to the main road and the layby where the bus stopped. I think I had done it in under two hours and I knew there was a bus every hour.

There was a woman waiting in the layby with a wee dog on a lead. I walked up and stood at the other end and looked back up towards the way the bus came so she didn't look at my face for too long. I could feel her staring at me and then I heard her shout 'Be about ten minutes son.' And I held up my hand to say thanks and carried on looking up the road.

I could hear her talking to the dog. It was a wee white terrier and she was going 'Loo-Loo, Loo-Loo, bus is coming Loo-Loo' to it in a high baby voice. I looked and the dog was wagging its tail and looking up at her and sort of dancing about all excited. The woman was old with short grey hair and big glasses. She grinned at me when I looked and said 'She loves the bus!' I went aye and nodded.

'Been hiking up the glen son?' she said coming a bit nearer me. And I said aye and tried to look down.

'Are ye a scout?'

I said aye and I thought 'Brilliant!'

Then we heard the bus coming and she said 'Oh here we go . . .'

I got a £4.80 return and found a seat on my own upstairs. It was nine miles into town and the road followed the river all the way down the valley.

The town was wee with one main street and lots of wee shops. It was busy, with loads of people and a farmers' market with stalls in the street selling cheese and candles and a Buffalo Burger van. I got off the bus and walked up and down the street looking at all the places I needed to get stuff and there was a Co-op and a wee bookshop that sold cards and pictures.

Nobody even looked at me. I bought belVitas, two loafs of bread, four tins of corned beef and four tins of beans, another Dundee cake and another cherry cake and a box of teabags and a bag of sugar. It weighed like hell in the backpack and I knew I'd never be able to get enough food for us for weeks and weeks or months. Maybe I'd have to keep coming back here once a week. I bought a big steak and ketchup for Peppa for a treat when I got back and in the health food shop I got more nuts and dried apricots. I also got a big bag of Bombay Mix for Peppa because she loves it. In a chemist I got soap and shampoo and plasters for the first aid kit.

In the bookshop there was a young woman with blond hair and an English accent and she saw me looking and said

'Are you looking for anything in particular?' and I said I wanted a book for my wee sister who was ten. She said 'Is she a good reader?' and I said aye.

And then she said 'What sort of thing does she like?' and I said she liked stories about Indians and people in wars and people going on adventures. I didn't look at her when I was speaking I just kept staring at the bookshelves. It smelled nice in there, like vanilla and sugar.

The woman said 'What about this?' and she showed me a book called *Treasure Island* that had pirates and a treasure chest and a sandy beach on the front. The woman said 'The language might be a bit strange for her at first but if she's a good reader she might like it. It's a classic.'

I said 'She's clever. She likes words.' I didn't say what kind of words.

The woman held up another book called *Kidnapped* with an old boat on the front and two men holding swords and wearing eighteenth-century clothes. 'This is by the same author and it's a fantastic adventure story.'

I got them both and they were £9.98 and I put them in the backpack. Now it was really heavy on my back and I had five miles to do when I got back to the forest, but I didn't think about it and did what it says in the SAS Survival Handbook about setting and achieving small goals minute by minute and not projecting as a way of keeping up morale in stressful survival situations.

So I went to the library and paid £4 for an hour's internet access on a PC.

I knew I was going to do this all the time and I knew deep in my mind that it was why I had really come to the town. To find out what had happened after we ran and where Maw was and where the polis and the social were looking for us.

There were loads of stories about us. I searched Google News and put in our names – Salmarina and Paula Brown.

The latest headlines were all SEARCH WIDENS FOR MISSING SCHOOLGIRLS and MISSING GIRLS – POLICE EXTEND SEARCH AREA.

I went back a week. I found SISTERS MISSING AFTER STEPDAD KILLING and DESPERATE MUM PLEADS FOR MISSING SISTERS TO COME BACK. There were pictures of Maw at a press conference crying and a full face photo of Robert. Further down there were pictures of me when I was ten in a red school sweatshirt and a picture of Peppa when she was eight. There was a picture from one of Maw's phones of me and Peppa staring, and Peppa was wearing her black fleece and I had a white T-shirt on and my hair was shorter.

I read the story about the press conference and it said Maw was pleading with us to come back and we were not in trouble and she just wanted to know we were safe. And the policeman said he believed we were in the area where we lived and may be being held or hidden by someone and that 'we are increasingly concerned about the safety of Salmarina and Paula'.

Then I found an STV video of people searching round our flats and along the wall and up to the lighthouse and by the shore. There were crowds all wearing hi-viz jackets and I saw Ian Leckie and Mhari and people who lived in our flats like Big Chris and Mrs Duggan with her dog on a lead. The voice said 'Concerned neighbours and friends took part in a search for the missing girls who vanished from the flat in Linlithgow Court on Wednesday morning. The body of their mother's partner Robert McColm was found in the flat after police were called by a neighbour. Police say he died from stab wounds. The girls' mother Claire

Brown, 29, was in the flat at the time of the girls' disappearance and it is still unclear how the sisters Salmarina, 13, and Paula, 10, left the flat. Police say they were last known to be in the flat on Tuesday night. Local volunteers scoured waste ground, parks and areas of the shore . . .'

I skipped down and found CCTV LEAD IN SEARCH FOR MISSING SISTERS and SCHOOL UNIFORM RIDDLE OF MISSING GIRLS from four days ago. There was footage of us at the train station in Glasgow, me with the big rucksack and Peppa with her backpack walking across by the shops in the school uniforms.

Then I started to feel a panic coming and my heart starting banging very fast and I felt like someone was squeezing my chest. I was just staring at the screen and the shot of us went all blurry. I wanted to breathe but I couldn't and I started to try to stand up and I staggered back into the chair and it went over with a big crash.

My eye was looking along the grey carpet down between metal shelves of books and black leather shoes were running towards me and a man was saying 'Alright, it's okay, it's okay.'

He was old and wearing a blue shirt and a tie and he crouched down beside me and I started panicking again. I hadn't minimised the screen so he'd see what I was looking at. But he was sitting me up and saying 'You feeling faint?' and I said aye. Then I said, 'I'm okay. I just tripped.'

I was trying to see round him to see if the CCTV of us was still on the screen. He made me sit with my head between my knees and he rubbed my back and went 'Just breathe . . . you're alright.'

I didn't want him to rub me and I wriggled out from his hand and got up still trying to see the screen and was going 'I'm fine, I'm fine, I need to go outside.'

He was looking right at me and smiling. His face was

big and he had a grey beard and little round glasses. He said 'Aye it is warm in here, go out and have a breath of air.'

He turned and then he looked straight at the page I had up with the CCTV footage of us. There was the blurry grey of me and Peppa and a time and date line and the headline underneath. He stood still for a minute and then he walked away smiling.

I stepped over to the PC and quit the page and deleted my search history then got the backpack and swung it onto my shoulder and the tins in it clanked and I walked straight out.

I walked up the street breathing deep and I felt really hungry and I wondered if that was why I fell and started blacking out. My head was racing with all the stuff on the internet about us and the guy seeing the page. If they searched and looked at what I was looking at they might guess who I was and I still didn't know what had happened to Maw. And I was worried about getting back for Peppa.

To calm down I went and got a Buffalo Burger and chips and a can of Coke and sat on a bench that looked out across the river and ate them. Buffalo tastes like beef. I got that lovely rushy feeling you get when you are really hungry and you eat and you want to dance about. And I felt better and calmer and my mind stopped racing and worrying. When you are hungry you get tense and your body produces adrenaline and other hormones that make you want to get food so that was what had happened to me I think.

I was going to have to take a risk and go back into the library. Sometimes you have to calculate the potential loss and gain of a decision when you cannot know the outcome and are risking something. Predatory fish like pike do this when they are hunting. It is a kind of calculation where they weigh the potential energy they will get from attacking a prey against the amount of energy it will take to attack it and the likelihood of them being successful, given certain variables like how far away the fish is, what kind of fish it is and even things like water temperature and flow. If the gain outweighs loss in the risk then they attack. When you think about it that is a very complex calculation. And pike do it in milliseconds with a really small brain. That is why big pike often only take very big lures or lures that create enough disturbance to appear like a big prey fish.

So I thought about it and went back to the library and when I went in the man with the beard was on the desk and he held up his hand and went 'Feeling better?' and I said aye and went to the terminal. I like old men, like him and Ian Leckie.

I had nearly thirty minutes left but I couldn't find anything about Maw in the news bits, I just found a thing from a paper that said THE CHAOTIC LIVES OF MISS- ING SISTERS and there was a picture of our flats and another picture of me and Peppa when we were wee and a big picture of Robert. One bit said 'The dead man, Robert McColm, 31, had been Claire Brown's partner for three years. Police say he was well known to them and had spent time in prison and had a string of convictions for theft, burglary and assault. Police sources confirm McColm had suffered stab wounds to the throat and was found in the bedroom of the oldest girl, Salmarina, when police entered the flat last Wednesday morning.' There was a picture of my school and the rector had said 'Salmarina is an intelligent and capable girl who received special support in the school's vulnerable learners unit.'

I read everything I could and searched Maw's name again. Then I thought of Twitter, because people always tweet stuff about murders that you don't get in the papers. When

I searched Maw on Twitter there were loads of tweets, lots of them by people who said they knew her or knew us. Mhari had tweeted on it loads of time. Hers went 'Prayin 4 there safety. God bless them both and keep them safe.' A woman called Blonde Iris said 'Just prayin 4 the lasses missing 7 days now.'

There were ones about Robert. One from GORDON-MAC said 'Robert McColm wus a horible wee shite an got wot he deservd. If the lassie did him it was coz he was abusing her.' People had retweeted it and there was a thread all about that. They said stuff like 'He wiz a fukin pedo. Hud it comin.'

Then I found one from ALISON@THECLUB from yesterday and it said 'Claire in rehab now getting dried out. In the Abbey. NHS are paying.'

Another on that thread said 'The Abbey is the best place for her now even with the lassies away. Claire needs to go into a recovery programme.' And that was Ian Leckie.

I searched 'rehab the abbey scotland' and found one called the Abbey and there was a picture on the website of an old stone house with a big lawn and trees in the sunshine. It said they offered detox and rehabilitation for people suffering from addiction problems and it followed the Twelve Step recovery programme. And it was in Galloway. I got the address and searched it on Google Maps and then Google Earth. It was twenty-six miles from the Forest Park and set back off a road. And that was where Maw was.

I printed out the map and the site page and then my hour expired and I paid for the print and went.

I got back to the layby on the main road at just after 3.00. It was five miles to go now and there was no way I'd do it in the light, but I started back through the car park and up the forestry road. There were two cars in the car park and as I was going up the forestry road a man and a woman both in cagoules and walking boots were coming back down and they nodded at me but I just kept looking down.

But I felt better. I had the food and Maw wasn't in the jail and there was nothing to say they were looking down here or even that they knew where we were. They knew about the school uniforms and knew we'd gone into Glasgow but that was it.

The backpack was heavy and I tried to get a slow rhythm walking and leaning forwards and breathing slow. It was overcast and dull and the wind was still from the west and it was still warm and all the snow was gone. My thoughts started to go slow.

Seeing the picture of Robert made me think about when I killed him.

I decided to do it just before Easter, the night I tried to block the door and stop him getting in and he was raging and he forced the chest of drawers out the way. I sat on the bed and he stood over me and went 'What did I say Sal? You got to be nice to me. If you don't I'll go see Peppa.'

And I said 'You fucking leave her.'

And he laughed and said 'She's getting old enough.'

And I said 'If you touch her I'll kill you. She'll fucking kill you and she'll tell Maw.'

And he laughed and started undoing his trousers.

Afterwards he fell asleep on my bed. He always did if he was drunk and I had to belt him and push him to get him off. That night after I'd been to the bathroom I looked at him and thought I could kill him. And the whole plan came into my mind. Getting the locks and fitting them. Running to the woods and surviving and making it so they couldn't blame Maw. I'd read a story about two kids who killed a woman and her daughter and they stabbed them in the throat because it stops you screaming. I already had the Bear Grylls knife then and I already knew loads about survival.

The next week I got the lock and put it on Peppa's door and I gave her a key and told her to lock herself in when she went to bed in case Robert was drunk and tried to get in. I didn't say why then but I told her later when I said I was going to kill him.

The problem was that I never knew when he was going to come in and I had to get everything ready and bought and arranged and the locks done on Maw's door. I got Mrs Kerr to show me how to read an Ordnance Survey map and plot with a compass and she nearly shat herself when I asked her and she went all gushy and kept saying 'This is marvellous Sal.' I told her I wanted to go orienteering and she showed me grid references and the lines of longitude and latitude and the way you use the compass and find north and then plot the direction you want to go. She also showed me contours and indications of gradient and how to tell what type of woodland there was.

Robert didn't come in every night. Sometimes it was weeks and weeks between it. Even when he and Maw had been drinking he didn't always come in and after Robert came Maw was drunk a lot more and there was a lot more weed and whizz and mandy in the flat.

But if I thought he'd stopped he hadn't. Sometimes he came in and was all quiet and whispered and called me 'darlin'' and sometimes he came in and just grabbed me and yanked me up and held my hair in his fist. He was strong and he twisted my hair. Sometimes afterwards he said things like 'You're very special to me, you know that?' and sometimes he just pushed me back onto the bed and walked out. I never looked at him or saw his eyes and they were always half closed anyway.

Sometimes he sat there afterwards and told me about not telling and about us getting taken away and split up and sometimes he talked like everything was normal and he handed me tissues and said things like 'I'm away to Glasgow the morra, bit of business' like I wanted to know. Once he sat on the end of my bed and started crying and saying sorry. He was really drunk that night and he leant over and fell asleep.

It took months to get everything we needed and I watched loads of YouTubes on everything. I had everything under my bed and I was always the first one up to get the post and packages. I had about twelve different emails for the Amazon accounts and I had so many usernames and passwords I had to write them down with the account numbers in a wee book I kept in my bedside drawer. I bought nuts and raisins and brioches in sealed bags and cake and belVitas that would keep.

It was the day Peppa's trainers and Helly Hansen waterproof and backpack arrived and I made her put them all under her bed and then I told her I was going to kill Robert. And she said 'You'll go to prison' and I told her I wouldn't and I told her the plan about running and surviving and she got excited. Then I told her about what he did with me at night and how he'd said he was going to start on her and she went really quiet and then she said 'Kill him Sal.'

For the next two weeks Peppa was excited about running all the time and kept coming up and saying in a low voice like in a film trailer 'We are going to survive!', and I told her to be quiet. She started watching Bear Grylls and Ray Mears on YouTube and I showed her the map and stuff about making a shelter and how we'd make a fire. I showed her the knife and she said 'Nice.' She packed her backpack ready and kept it under her bed and I let her try on the school uniform and then we hid it.

The Saturday before we ran Maw and Robert didn't come home and in the morning I got Peppa's breakfast and she went off to gymnastics and I put the lock on Maw's door and cleared all the shavings and sawdust up. The lock worked and I put the key under the council recycling box in the hall. Maw and Robert got back in the afternoon when I was watching YouTubes and Maw sat in the front room and drank cider and Robert smoked weed in front of the telly.

That night Robert came into my room and he was rough and angry and kept saying 'Oh you little bitch' to me. I wanted to do it that night but the next day was Sunday and it was no good trying to run on a Sunday. All the train and bus times I'd got were for the week.

But I knew it was going to be soon because I kept feeling calm when I thought about it and I wasn't panicking at all. It was October so there would still be some leaf cover in the woods and there was still a good chance of catching fish. The weather forecast for that week said it was going to be clear and cold with a northerly wind moving in towards the end of the week.

I told Peppa it was going to be that week and we carried on like normal on Monday. I got her up and got her breakfast and we both went to school and Maw went to the club in the afternoon and Robert was in the flat and not going away. On Monday night when they were out I found another forty quid in his drawer and took it. On the Tuesday I started dumping all the cards and the laptop and the phones I'd been using. I took out the SIMs and threw them into the sea off the wall. I chucked in the book with all the passwords and usernames because I had got everything we needed. On the way back I saw Ian Leckie coming down the shorefront and he said 'How's ma Bonny Sal?' and I said fine and he asked about Maw and gave me ten quid for chips for me and Peppa.

Robert and Maw went out on Tuesday night and got back about 11.00 and there was a bit of shouting and banging and then it went quiet and I knew Maw was passed out and I could hear the telly and I sat in my room waiting. Then the telly went off and Robert came in and said 'Alright darlin' – your maw's out of it.' He was drunk and stoned and kept staring at me with a grin on his face and I sat on the edge of the bed. He stank of drink and fags and the incense sticks they burned and he leant onto me still grinning.

Afterwards he was still grinning and he lay on his side on the bed and was saying things to himself in a little quiet voice. He was wearing his pants and his jeans were on the floor. I went into the bathroom and washed my face and then got the key from under the recycling box. I opened Maw's door and she was lying face down on her bed. Her mobile was on the bedside table and I went in and checked it had charge. Then I locked her in and put the key in front of the door on the hall carpet.

I went back to my room and it was quiet and dim with just my bed light on and Robert was asleep and breathing slow. I felt under the bed and got the knife and stood over him, behind him on the other side of my bed with the knife pointing down in my left fist over his neck. I did slow breathing and tried to centre myself and felt the breath coming in and lifting my diaphragm and my belly going in a bit. I felt the breath coming out and my belly going out and I just made myself aware of that.

I stabbed him three times. The first was straight into his

windpipe and the knife went through and into the bed underneath and Robert's eyes opened and his mouth opened and he went 'ock'. The second was slightly further out and cut his throat right across and blood spat out in a stream and hit the wall and there was a hissing and whizzing sound coming from Robert. On the third I stabbed harder and felt the knife go through muscle and hit a bone which was probably his spine. The blood gushed and pumped out onto the bed and up the wall and I stepped back and I had blood up my arms and could feel it on my face.

Robert's mouth was open and his eyes had gone wide and you could see all the yellow in them. In his throat there was a big round black hole and his head was hanging back. He was still and then he jerked and blood gurgled out of the hole in his neck.

I stood there for five full minutes which I counted using elephants. Robert made another 'ock' sound and then he didn't move. Blood had soaked into the whole bed and it was all red.

I went through and had a shower and washed the knife off and then I dried myself and put my clothes in the washing and went back into my room and got clean pants and socks and a vest. I didn't look at Robert and I closed my door so Peppa wouldn't see in, then I went and banged on her door and she came out. She'd been asleep and I said 'We're going in the morning.'

She said 'Is Robert dead?' and I said 'Aye' and she said 'Was it easy?' and I said 'Aye.' She asked if Maw was alright and I said she was in her room asleep.

I got the rucksack and checked all the stuff and Peppa brought her backpack out and we put on the tights and skirts and blouses from the school uniform and then Peppa got her quilt and went through and slept on the sofa. I sat in the chair in the front room watching her sleep and set my alarm on the phone for 5.30 a.m.

It was dark by the time I got to the climb up towards our woods but there was a moon and it kept appearing from behind the clouds that were running along on the west wind. I went slow and sometimes I stopped and put the backpack down and stretched and flexed my shoulders. When the moon came out it was bright and clear and I could see everything in silver and grey. I heard a tawny owl screeching along by the plantation woods and as I climbed the steep bank up to our woods three deer jumped out of the bracken and bounded up away from me. When the cloud went over the moon it was almost too dark to see and I walked slower and tried to feel what was in front of me. It took a long time to get up to the start of the birch and pine in our woods and I was puffing and breathing hard lugging that backpack.

The clouds cleared again and the moon was bright as I got to our woods and there were sharp shadows of trees and diamond patches of silver light on the ground. The trees waved in the breeze and the light patches stretched and closed. The trees sounded like someone shuffling cards and there was my steps on the leaves and sometimes twigs cracking.

I could smell the fire from a way off and as I got nearer I saw a very faint glow and the round shape of the bender through the trees. Peppa had kept the fire going all day. I called 'Peppa!' as I came up to the bender and I heard her shout 'Yo Sal!' and she came running out and we hugged. The fire was going well and there was a new stack of wood by it.

'You've been away for ages. I was getting worried about you.'

'I was worried about you' I said.

'Did ye get me a book?'

'Aye. I got you two. And a steak.'

She poked the sticks on the fire into a blaze and I started unpacking the backpack. I showed her the books and she got a head torch and looked at them and then started reading *Kidnapped* while I put the kettle on.

I said 'Were you okay? Did you see anybody?'

And she kept on reading and then she looked up and said 'Aye. I met a lady. She made me a fire because mine had gone out. She's called Ingrid.'

Chapter Seven

Ingrid

Peppa told me what happened. She slept a lot after I left and then she tried to cut up the rabbit skins and make a hat but she couldn't get the needle through the skins right and she cut all the bits wrong and she said it looked like a rabbit that had been in a blender when she'd finished. Then she tried to get the fire going but couldn't get the little sticks started off the embers. She drank some boiled water from the kettle and ate a brioche and almonds and raisins and then she fell asleep again.

When she woke up there was a woman squatting in the entrance of the bender and looking at her. She jumped and panicked and wondered if she should shoot her with the airgun but the woman was smiling and holding a bunch of birch bark and pointing at the fire.

The woman was old and had long grey hair and was wearing a long, long coat all the way to the ground made of waxy cloth and had scarves tied up in her hair. Her face was flat and she had a small nose and eyes like she was Chinese. She had big white teeth and was wearing red lipstick and had bangles and beads on her wrists. There was a wee white scar on her cheekbone just under her eye in the shape of a crescent moon.

But she was smiling and saying things to Peppa in a foreign language and she started blowing at the embers of the fire and then she shredded up the birch bark and got a striker and flint out and made sparks and got an ember going just like I did. She blew it and fed it with bark and twigs and burned ends. And then she said something else foreign and walked off into the wood.

Peppa didn't know whether to run or not and she sat on the bed in the bender wishing she had a phone so she could phone me and ask what to do. Then the woman came back with a stack of sticks and some bigger bits of wood and she snapped the longer branches up and got the fire going.

Then she went 'Good?' to Peppa and Peppa said thanks.

The woman went off again and Peppa could hear her pulling sticks out of the undergrowth and snapping branches. And all the time she was talking and muttering and some-times she laughed like there was someone else there. Peppa came out of the bender and watched her. She was bundling sticks and wood under her arm and striding about pulling and snapping and muttering all in her language.

The woman came back and made a pyramid fire and then started stacking more wood next to it and Peppa sat by it and the woman watched the fire burning for a bit and then said 'Good' again. Then she went off to get more wood and eventually there was a huge pile all snapped to the right length stacked by the fire.

Peppa didn't feel scared of the woman and she didn't think she'd tell on us so she put the kettle on and said 'Are you wanting a cup a tea?' and the woman said 'Yah, tea' and sat down opposite Peppa and warmed her hands. The kettle boiled and Peppa made her tea with milk and sugar in it like we have and the woman drank it and said 'Good.'

Peppa said 'Can you speak English?'

And the woman said 'Yes I can. My name is Ingrid. I am a doctor. I prefer to speak German. Can you speak German?' and Peppa said she didn't and the woman said 'Then I shall teach you.'

And then the woman said 'I too live in a bender. Mine is larger and better constructed than yours.'

Peppa said 'My sister made it. She's gone to town to get food.'

And then the woman stood up and said 'Good. Thank you for the tea. Do not allow the fire to go out again. You now have a plentiful supply of wood.'

And off she went.

Peppa told me all this the night I got back when she was eating the steak I got her and I had corned beef and we both had beans. I started to worry about Ingrid because now someone knew where we were and they could tell, and if people came looking for us and asked, they might say 'Aye there are two lassies living in a bender up there in the woods.'

But Peppa said she wouldn't and that we could trust her because she lived in a bender too and she was out on her own in the woods and she didn't look like a wanky walker in a cagoule and walking boots. In fact she sounded like she looked like a witch and I said that and Peppa said 'Aye she did.' But Peppa seemed to trust her and she was okay about it so I thought I wouldn't worry. I was really tired after walking all the way back with the food so I left off telling Peppa about the stuff on the internet till tomorrow and we stacked up the fire and went to bed.

Because Ingrid spoke German and looked like a witch

it made me think of the Nachthexen in the Second World War at the Battle of Stalingrad which is my favourite battle in a war. Nachthexen means 'night witches' in German and it was the name the Germans gave to the women who flew Russian bombers at night and attacked them. So I told Peppa about them and I had told her before but she likes it.

They were a women-only squadron of bombers and they flew really old flimsy biplanes made of cloth and wood and they could only carry six bombs at a time. They flew slow, but the little biplanes could dodge the German guns and fighter planes and then they went so slow that the German planes stalled which means their engines stopped working in the air. Also the Nachthexen used to shut their engines off when they were coming in at night low over the Germans so they didn't hear them and they could drop bombs right on them. The Germans thought the sound of the wind on the gliding planes was like a witch's broom. They killed loads and loads of Germans which is fair because Germany had invaded their country and killed loads of Russians and they started the war and they murdered all the Jews. The German soldiers were so scared of the Russian women they called them Nachthexen and they thought they were witches and demons because nobody else dared to fly at night and bomb them so they thought they were magic. This happened in 1942 and 1943 when they were fighting over Stalingrad which was a city in southern Russia that is now called Volgograd. I saw a film called *Enemy at the Gates* about snipers in the battle that I really liked and then I read about it on Wikipedia. Peppa fell asleep when I was telling her all this stuff and we were both really warm.

The next day we went to the loch fishing for pike with the plugs and wire traces. It was sunny and it felt warm in the sun and the wind was only light. As we walked down I told her about the internet stuff and Maw in a rehab, and about the papers and the search for us and the CCTV. She was worried about Maw but I said it was good they were going to try and dry her out and stop her drinking and she wasn't in jail so they knew she didn't kill Robert.

Peppa said 'What will happen if they find us?' I said 'I'll get arrested and charged with killing Robert and you'll get put in care.'

And she got upset then and bit her bottom lip and looked down and stopped walking. Then she said 'But I'm glad you killed Robert.' And I said 'I know' and she said 'You can just tell them why you did it and why we ran and they might let you go.'

I'd thought of that too. I'd thought about telling about Robert before, and him saying he was going to go in Peppa's room and him hitting Maw and being drunk and stoned all the time. But I knew the first thing that would happen would be he'd get arrested and we'd get taken and split up because that was what always happened. Plus nobody would believe Maw didn't know and she might get charged with abuse or neglecting us and go to jail. I had read stories about it on news websites, where the mother got charged and went to jail and the stepdad went for longer because he was the one who did all the bad stuff like killing a baby or starving a little girl, but they said the mother let it happen and she got done too. They always blame the mother of any kid who gets abused or hurt, but it is always the man who does it.

Peppa said 'Can we go and get Maw? You said we'd get her and she could come and live with us in the forest.'

'Aye but not now Peppa. She needs to get better from

drinking. She needs to go into a recovery programme. Ian Leckie said that in his tweet.'

'When she's better will we get her?'

I said 'Aye we will' but I didn't know how.

I had explained to Peppa about Maw having a disease called alcoholism which is an addiction to alcohol that makes you stop being normal and makes you need to drink all the time like Maw, and fall asleep and cry and not look after your kids. It also makes you accept the unacceptable in other people and have a high tolerance of inappropriate behaviour it said on one of the websites I read about it. Like with Robert. She just let him hit her and take her money and hit us because she had a disease that made her think it was alright. It is caused by having a different chemistry in your brain that makes you want and crave the thing that is making you ill and you don't even know you've got it and you deny you're ill. Maw used to go 'I just need a wee drink Sal to make me calm down' and I'd go and get a can or a bottle of cider I'd hidden for her. She called it a 'wee drink' but it was never a wee drink.

If they got us and I got charged with killing Robert they would charge me with murder not culpable homicide because they would know I had planned it and in Scottish law if you plan it and arrange it you can only be charged with murder and that would be a life sentence of at least about twenty years in prison. So even if I told them why I did it, it wouldn't matter because the law in Scotland says if you plan it then it is murder. And I planned it for months. I read a lot about doing a murder and charges and the way they put you on trial and defences. The only defence I would have is that I am mad and I didn't know what I was doing was wrong. But I am not mad and I knew it was against the law and I still did it. And I don't think it was wrong. If someone is going to destroy everything and doesn't care, or if they want to pull everybody else into their own evil then you have to kill them. When I was stabbing Robert I felt calm and happy and I knew it was right. Like the Nachthexen had to kill the Germans.

Peppa ran on down to the loch through the bracken and past the warren where we got the first rabbit. Bright sunshine is not good for pike fishing and they stay in the shade so we walked along the beach and climbed along the loch edge to where there were trees and overhanging branches putting shade in the water. There was a big tree that had toppled in and it was half under and that was a good place for pike which are ambush predators and wait in weeds or submerged trees to dart out at little fish going past.

I set up the rod and tied on a trace and a plug which was white with a red head and had a rattle in it which sends out soundwaves that attract pike. I showed Peppa how to take off the bail arm and hold the line with one finger, then bring the rod back and flick it forwards, aiming at the sky if you wanted it to go far and then point the rod after the plug as it went through the air. She tried a few and got it and started flicking the plug out and wobbling it back along by the tree. I sat and watched her and thought about how to cook a pike if we got one. They are bony and you have to try to get the backbone out but I could do that with my Bear Grylls knife.

Peppa said 'I think it's stuck Sal', and she was trying to wind the reel in and it wasn't turning and the line was tight all the way out to by the tree. Then there was a huge splash and a swirl on the water and Peppa fell back on her bum still holding the rod and shouted 'Sal I've got one.'

The rod was bending right over and the line was cutting and zooming across the water away from the tree and I said

'Reel it in Peppa!' and she started trying to reel it but it was too strong, and the rod kept jerking and banging where it was fighting. It was a big one. Peppa said 'Sal you do it' and I took the rod off her and felt the weight and the tugging of the fish through it and the spool was spinning and taking line off where the pike was running away out into the loch. The line was only ten pound which is 4.5 kilos and I was scared the pike was heavier than that and it would snap it, but it held and I got the rod up high and let it absorb the bucks and kicks from the pike, then I reeled in as hard as I could and the pike jumped and we saw it flash out and curl above the water, all gold and yellow in the sunshine. Peppa went 'It's a fucking monster!' and it was. It splashed back in and I kept the line taut and reeled in more. I said 'We're gonna get this Peppa' and I reeled in more.

It was close in now and we could see it going like a torpedo with the plug in its mouth and the line cutting through the water to the rod. I kept reeling and it seemed to stop pulling and jerking the closer it got to the shore. I shouted to Peppa to get a stick and she ran into the trees and I could hear her crashing and snapping in there. I walked backwards up the beach and started to drag the pike up out of the water, and the line was so tight it was pinging and twanging with the weight of it. I dragged it so only its tail was still in the water. And it was big. Its head was the size of mine and its mouth could've taken it all in. It looked like it was grinning at us. Peppa ran up with a stick about two foot long she'd snapped off a tree, and I put the rod down and got the stick and swung it back as far as I could and belted the pike on the back of the head as hard as I could.

With the smack of the stick it went all tense and then shuddered and whacked its tail back and forth. The plug was hooked into its mouth by both trebles at the side. The pike shuddered again and then it went still but its eyes were open and it grinned.

Peppa went 'Bloody hell Sal.'

She knelt down next to it and put her hand out to touch its head. I was just going to say 'Don't' when the pike suddenly turned its head and opened its mouth and snapped. Peppa sprang back and screamed, clutching her hand and wrist, and I saw blood spurt out from it and she screamed again and I hit the pike again.

Peppa was hopping along the shore holding her hand and shouting 'It fucking bit me. It bit me. Bastard!' I ran to her and looked and there were three long slashes streaming blood down her hand and onto her wrist. I breathed and told myself not to panic but my heart was slamming and I felt dizzy when I saw her blood. It was pouring out and dripping on the stones. She was holding her hand out and screaming as it bled and red was running down her arm and onto her T-shirt.

I said 'Hold it up and squeeze above your wrist' and I pulled off my fleece and vest and ripped the vest open. She was going 'Aaah bastard!'

I got her hand and bound it as hard as I could with the vest, round and round as tight as I could get it and she was going 'It's sore Sal, it's sore.' Some blood was coming out from under the vest and a patch of red was swelling up in the middle. I said 'Keep it high' and she held it up above her head and blood dripped down her arm. I got her to sit and breathe deep and keep her hand up and the blood seemed to stop and there was just a patch the size of a 50p in the middle of the vest. I got one of my laces out of my trainers and pulled my fleece back on and then I bound the lace round her forearm to make a tourniquet and stop the bleeding. I kept saying 'It's alright Peppa, it's alright.'

She said 'Will I bleed to death?' and I said she was being

daft. She said 'I thought it was dead', and I said 'So did I. It is now.' And we looked back up the beach and it was on its side, still, with its silver belly towards us.

'That is one big bastard' said Peppa.

'I should've brought the first aid kit. I will next time' I said.

I told her to stay where she was and keep her hand up and I went and kicked the pike to make sure it was dead and it jerked a bit and then went still again and I got the hooks out and wound in the plug onto the rod. Then I got my knife and cut its head off and it was big and heavy and I had to push with all my weight to get the knife through its backbone. Then I gutted it and it was full of spawn in big lumps that looked like orange peel.

I chucked the guts and the head into the loch and then I got the rod and lugged the pike up over onto my shoulder. Even without its head it was as long as my legs.

Pike have razor sharp teeth that grow in rows and can cut through even thick fishing line. The teeth have an anti-coagulant on them which makes wounds bleed a lot and stops them clotting. This is to help them hunt because they can bite and injure a fish and then just watch it bleed to death before they eat it. Peppa was right. They are bastards.

I carried the pike and the rod and Peppa walked up slowly from the loch holding her hand up. She kept stopping and saying 'It's throbbing Sal' and I just walked with her. The sun had gone in and it started spitting rain on a westerly breeze and off over the loch the clouds were dark. It took a long time to get back up to the bender and by the time we got there it was raining hard and we were both soaked and the fire had gone out.

I dumped the pike and got Peppa into the bender and got her Helly Hansen and put it on her and let her lie there.

The wood pile had got soaked and I was angry that I hadn't stacked some inside to stay dry when we went off. A lot of survival is planning, stopping, thinking and planning and trying to see what can go wrong and thinking about what will happen if things change. I hadn't done that in the morning because the sun was out and Peppa was excited about fishing and I was happy because I'd got back safe from town and was with her again and we were still free. So I didn't stop and think before we left and that was a lesson for me because now we were cold and wet and didn't have a fire.

I couldn't make a fire in the place we had it and I had to try and start a small one in the entrance of the bender where the rain couldn't get it. I found a few drier sticks in the bottom of the pile and stacked the rest in the bender to dry. Then I found some twigs and leaves and dry grass in the bender that was still dry and made a tinder bundle. You have to strike the steel and flint and get a big spark onto the tinder and then let it smoulder a bit and then blow it slow and steady until it grows and glows, and then if you keep blowing air through it, it will burst into flame and you can lay it down and use small dry twigs and grass to get it going. I had seen it done loads of times on YouTube and so far I'd had no trouble with the fire.

But the tinder was still a bit damp and I couldn't get the spark to take. I struck and struck and struck and big flashing sparks dropped down onto the bundle but nothing took. Peppa was just lying on the bed watching and she said 'Sal I'm hungry.'

I stopped and got her some cake and bread and nuts and dried apricots from the backpack. We had a bit of boiled water in the kettle and I got her a drink of water. After she'd eaten she said she was cold and she got into the sleeping bag and pulled the blankets over her.

I kept on at the tinder with the striker and wished I'd brought a lighter or some firelighters. Fire isn't just good for cooking and staying warm it's good for your spirit. When we got here all those days ago I was tense and angry and doubting everything we'd done and I was getting snappy with Peppa when I was doing the first shelter. But as soon as we got the fire going I felt better. Just sitting and looking into it and feeling the heat makes you calm and you feel like you belong where you are. And sitting there on the first night by the fire I felt like what we'd done was right and killing Robert was right and everything would work out for us. And that was the fire that made me feel that. That's why you can't neglect your fire like I'd done that morning.

I was striking and striking and the rain was hammering down now and splashing in onto my legs and onto the spot where I wanted to make the fire. I went further in and brushed the ground dry of leaves and twigs down to the soil. I kept on striking and letting the sparks drop onto the tinder bundle but it was still not taking. Sometimes a little ember would start and glow and then just go out. Every time it did I felt worse and every strike that didn't work made me feel more sad and tired.

In a crisis in survival you have to stop and think and plan. The SAS Survival Handbook says the most important factor in long-term survival is attitude. The way you think affects your chances of thriving. If you are negative and only think things are going to get worse or you can't go on then you will start acting like that. And the more you think and act like that the worse things get and the more you make bad decisions. And that is when you have to stop and think and plan and take action to make the situation better. Even a small thing can help.

So I stopped striking and got my waterproof and got up from sitting and looked at Peppa and she was asleep and her sore hand was sticking out from the blankets with the vest still tied on it and the tourniquet. I loosened the tourniquet and felt her fingers and they were really cold. I slid my hand down her back inside her clothes and her back was warm. So I tucked her up in the blankets and then I went out into the rain with my hood up.

I needed to walk and think and I went up from the bender where the slope starts with birch and spruce. I climbed up, slipping a bit on the wet leaves, and carried on along a deer path through the spruce. Further up there were really tall larches with big spaces under them covered in yellow needles. Larch is a coniferous tree which changes in winter and sheds its old needles and then grows new green ones in spring. It goes the colour of butter in autumn and grows straight and very strong and they used to use it to make ships' masts.

The rain was still coming down hard and I climbed over a little ridge of rocks all covered in brambles and ferns and came up on a flat bit where there were big spruce with branches that spread right out like huge skirts around the tree and were very deep green and glistening in the rain. Spruce is brilliant for waterproofing shelters and you can use the base of one for a shelter by taking out a few lower branches and using the ones above for a roof. I thought I'd cut some to try to make a platform of spruce branches to go high up over our fire and keep the worst of the rain off it. You need some long poles to make a base about two metres up above the fire between the trees and then you pile on spruce branches and they stop the rain getting on the fire below. I'd seen Ed Stafford make one when he was marooned in the Okavango Delta and it had kept his fire dry even in the African rainy season. I'd also seen him dry a tinder bundle by stuffing it down his pants for a day and letting his body heat dry the damp out of it. I wondered if I should've tried that.

I pushed my way into a big spruce and started cutting out lower branches with my knife. Inside the branches by the trunk of the tree it was completely dry and the twigs on the branches snapped like Twiglets. Even though the rain was hammering down just outside, the inside of the tree stayed bone dry. That's how waterproof the needles on the branches are. I snapped loads of twigs off them and filled the pockets of my jacket with them. Then I saw a bundle of dry twigs in a ball just where one of the branches met the trunk above my head. I pulled it down and it was a bird's nest. It had a little hollow in the middle of it lined with soft dry grass and little white downy feathers. It was thin spruce twigs all woven and tangled together into a ball. It was lovely and I held it in my hands. It must've been from a migratory bird that came to the forest for the summer and was now somewhere like Africa. She spent the whole summer making it and having her eggs in it and feeding the fledglings and teaching them to fly.

But it was also really dry and brilliant for tinder so I stuffed it in my jacket and got all the spruce boughs and dragged them back to the bender. Then I got some long dead poles of larch and wedged them up between the trees outside the bender. I made a kind of triangle frame as far as I could reach up, which was about two and a half metres above where we had the fire outside the entrance to the bender. It was still raining but the damp and slime on the tree bark helped me slide the poles between the tree trunks and set them horizontal. Then I criss-crossed smaller branches over it to make a roof and then I piled all the spruce branches up on it so they lay flat and didn't let any light through. And it worked. The rain was still coming down straight and hard all around but the spot under it with the ashes from our fire was covered. It was like an umbrella. I got rocks then and made a platform to keep the fire off wet ground and then I put the bird's nest on the rock and got the striker. I got a spark that took with the third strike and I blew the ember and it glowed and I blew more and got a flame.

I piled on the dry twigs and it was soon going well and I used the dry sticks from the bender to make the pyramid and I stacked more sticks by it to dry in its heat.

I sat on a rock and watched it starting to fire flames up and pump out smoke and crackle and spit. I said thank you to the bird for the nest.

I got water from the burn and set the kettle on the frame to boil and set more wood to dry by the fire and then I got the first aid kit.

Peppa was still sleeping but her arm was outside the blankets. I put on a head torch so I could see and I took off the tourniquet and slowly unwrapped the vest round her hand. She had three long slashes going right down her hand and onto her wrist and the blood was going thick along them but her hand and wrist were pale and clammy and the skin was crinkly and white like it had been in a swim-ming pool for a long time. She stayed asleep while I washed them down with cotton wool and boiled water. There were little red lines running up her arm away from the cuts that looked like they had been done with a red pen. I was starting to worry about infection so I got the iodine and dabbed it all along the cuts and her skin went yellow. And that woke her up and she jerked away from me and screamed.

'I've got to Peppa or it'll get infected' I said.

She screwed her eyes up and bit her bottom lip while

I cleaned it with the iodine and she kept going 'Sore . . . sore Sal . . . sore.'

I got her two ibuprofen and codeine from the first aid kit and made her take them with water. They are really good painkillers and they would also make her drowsy which is good because her body needed to rest while it healed itself from the cut.

I put cotton wool across the cuts and then bandaged it up. I moved across so she could see out and see the fire.

'Look. I made a fire in a rainstorm' I said and she smiled. 'I made an umbrella to keep the rain off it.'

She said 'Clever Sal.'

Then I made tea for us with milk and sugar and I opened another can of beans and we had beans and bread and cake. It was getting dark now and the rain was easing off a bit and I stacked up wood on the fire to keep it going and left more drying by it. I got the pike and I hung it up over the fire with paracord from the frame to see if it would smoke and cook slow overnight.

Peppa was drifting off into sleep and I got my things off and got in behind her and we snuggled down while it got dark and the rain dripped outside and the fire hissed.

Chapter Eight

Fever

Peppa had a fever in the morning and she woke me wriggling and sweating. I got out of bed and got the fire going from the embers. The rain had stopped and I boiled water then got the vest and washed it out and soaked it and mopped Peppa's forehead to cool it. And she was burning and writhing about and I had a panic pain in my chest and belly.

She kept waking up a little bit and looking up and then closing her eyes again. Sometimes she muttered and said things I didn't understand. I tried to get her to drink water but she wouldn't and kept going floppy and falling asleep.

I got the fire banked up with wood and then went and collected more. I went back and unwrapped her bandage. The red lines were going all the way up her arm now and all around the cut was swollen and red and there was pus in the cuts.

I cleaned them all out again and used the iodine to disinfect it all and she didn't even wake up. I put on a new bandage and cotton wool over it all. Her fingers were swelling too and the red lines were darker and nearer purple. I knew this was an infection from the pike bite so I decided to give her an Amoxicillin which is an antibiotic and then made sure she had plenty of water and she was warm.

I had to shake her awake and she opened her eyes and stared at me all glassy, like she was drunk. She was all wet with sweat but she felt cold and clammy. I put her purple jumper on her and she just let me and then I sat her up and made her swallow the antibiotic pill. Then I wrapped her up warm again and sat next to her,

She opened her eyes again and said 'Sal I'm ill.'

I said 'I know but you'll be alright. You've got an infection from the pike bite and I've given you an Amoxicillin.' And she smiled and said 'Good' and then she went back to sleep.

It was colder that morning and the sun was out but there was a bit of frost on the leaves and twigs around our camp. The pike was all blackened with smoke and was dripping little lines of white liquid onto the fire that hissed. The skin was getting crispy and you could see the white flesh underneath.

I boiled the kettle and made tea for us both with the last milk we had and sugar. Peppa didn't want tea but she drank a bit more water and then started pulling all the blankets off her and jerking about and I mopped her head again because she was burning up.

Then she stopped and flopped down asleep again and I covered her. I sat by her for hours then. I only got up to feed the fire and once to go and have a pee. I wanted a phone or a tablet so I could find out about infection from pike bites and if there was some kind of bacteria she had got and how I could kill it. The Amoxicillin packet said to take one two times a day and I had three left.

There was no way of getting a phone or a tablet and

the only way I could get online was to go to the library again and that was too far and I couldn't leave Peppa on her own. She woke after a couple of hours and wanted water and she seemed more awake and said she was hungry so I gave her corned beef and beans. I boiled the kettle and made her pine needle tea from the long needles off Scots pine because it has got vitamin C in it. She liked it because I put sugar with it.

I undid the bandage again and it had swelled up more and the red lines were still there and there was more pus. I cleaned it all up and she screamed again when I put on the iodine. She wasn't as hot but she said she was tired and she went back to sleep.

I sat and thought about what to do. I had tried to plan for something like this by bringing the antibiotics but I didn't get enough and I didn't know if the four I had would work. I couldn't plan for the pike bite but I knew it was what was making her ill.

I always looked after Peppa when she was ill and I used to give her Calpol when she was a baby if she was teething or was getting hot, and I was only about four but Maw couldn't do that stuff with her or me. Sometimes because she was drunk and sometimes because she panicked and started crying if we were ill or we hurt ourselves and then she got drunk and went asleep.

When she got the letter that I was going in the vulnerable learners' unit at school she panicked because she said they were saying I was retarded. I got put it in after P7 because I couldn't write properly. Letters and words. I could read fine but when I wrote it looked like I was retarded. It didn't matter what I was thinking, when I wrote the words they came out different and spelled all wrong and looked like another language. Sometimes I could write something and then five minutes later even I couldn't understand what I'd written and neither could anybody else. It was better if I typed but even then sometimes I spelled words like I was pissed. Peppa had good writing and she could spell everything. I saw two reports they sent about me. One said I was above average intelligence but suffering from severe dyslexia and an inability to recognise phoneme clusters and patterns. The other said I was of high intelligence and had an advanced reading age but suffered from severe cognitive impairment when it came to writing and remembering the spelling of words. It said I would need learning support and a scribe in exams.

I think I can't write properly and I am very dyslexic because I am left-handed. And statistically if you are a girl and you are left-handed you are much more likely to be dyslexic, probably because your brain works the wrong way round from other people.

I also got put in the unit because I never smiled, and stared at people, and other kids called me weird and they were worried I'd get bullied in the main school which was big and had about 2,500 kids in it. The report said I was 'withdrawn, appeared socially isolated and seemed reluctant to form new friendships'. Which was true. I was like that. I still am.

I didn't have any friends in school and Peppa was still at primary. I stopped being friends with Mhari when I was about ten and she started going around with two other girls who thought I was weird and didn't live near us.

Maw never went to the meetings at school about me and she gave the letters they sent to me to read. Most of the other kids in the unit were headcases who hit teachers and threw things across classrooms. And there was also the

Bloy twins who were two fat girls from a big family called the Bloys who were all headbangers and druggies and in gangs. The twins were a year older than me and they never spoke either but they battered kids all over the school and when they walked down the corridors everyone got out of their way. They both wore the same clothes and gold chains and shell suits and Nikes.

But they never bothered me and neither did any kids at school because I was tall and I stared and other kids thought I was hard. And I am hard. I've never had a proper fight but I'm not scared of anybody. The only lessons I went to with normal kids were maths and geography because I liked them. The others kids in the class just sat on their phones all the lesson but I did the worksheets and read about glaciation and Third World poverty and climate change.

Most kids are on their phones all the time because they can Snapchat and Instagram each other and look at porn. The internet is mostly for porn and sending pictures, but there is a lot of good stuff with information and finding out about history and YouTube videos for when you need to know how to do things or fix things. Most things I need to know are on YouTube and there are documentaries too about history and I know a lot of stuff from it. And you can also buy things online which is what I did.

There was one boy in the unit I liked and sometimes had a laugh with. He was called Davy Mack and he was little and had pointy ears like a pixie and he smelled of fags and bubble gum. The only time I ever got a row in school was when he nicked a wheelchair from the disabled unit and pushed me all around the school corridors going really fast and screaming and shouting swear words. I liked it and it made me laugh flying along in the chair with wee Davy pushing me. We got caught by Mr Connor the deputy rector and Davy got excluded for two weeks and I got confined to the unit and wasn't allowed to go to maths and geography for a while.

The teacher in the unit was called Mrs Finlayson and she was quite old and little and she was nice and she sometimes looked into my eyes smiling, and once she said 'There's a lot going on in there isn't there Sal?'

Once a week we sat on the sofas in the quiet room and I had to tell her about my feelings. I couldn't tell her anything about the flat or Maw or Robert so I used to say I felt fine and I was happy and sometimes I made up things I was worried about because she seemed to want me to feel worried about something. I once told her I was worried about climate change and I am a bit because we are right on the firth on the coast and if global warming makes sea levels rise by a metre then the shore road and Ian Leckie's house and the wee shops by the wall would all get flooded. Our flats are on a hill up from town so we'd be alright. Mrs Finlayson nodded and said 'Well, it's something that we all need to think about . . .' I told her about people I loved – Peppa and Maw and Ian Leckie – and I never told her anything about Robert or even said his name to her.

Peppa woke up again when it started to get dark and I gave her another Amoxicillin and made more pine needle tea. She sat up in the bed and said her arm was sore and I did the bandage again, but I only had one bandage left so I reused the one I took off. There was still pus and it was still red and swollen up and the cuts seemed to be wider. She said it was really sore and it felt heavy and it throbbed.

I gave her cake and nuts and raisins to eat because she

said she didn't want to eat the pike. I ate a bit of it and the meat was white and tasted of smoke and it had a lot of bones in it. I gave Peppa a head torch and she read her book a bit and I got a head torch and went off into the woods to get more sticks and wood for the fire and to fill the kettle at the burn.

When I got back Peppa said she needed the toilet and I took her outside and she had diarrhoea which sometimes happens when you take antibiotics so I knew I'd have to make sure she had fluids and salt and sugar. I had to clean her up with the grass and I also used the vest soaked in boiled water, but it was getting cold so I got her back into bed and wrapped up. Her arm was still sore and swollen up and I gave her another ibuprofen and codeine. I sat and worried while she went back to sleep. I got the fire all stacked up with wood and sat watching it from the entrance of the bender for a long time. I kept the water hot and woke Peppa every two hours so she could have pine needle tea with a bit of salt and sugar in it.

It got really cold. The sky was clear and there was a bright three-quarter moon that made everything silver and grey in the woods and I watched frost form and sparkle on the leaves and twigs on the ground. I stayed warm by the fire and Peppa stayed in the bed. Her temperature was down and she wasn't kicking and jerking in her sleep, so that was good.

But we had a bad night. I didn't really sleep, I just sat watching the fire and checking on Peppa and I got one blanket and wrapped it around me. In the night I heard the owl shriek and I heard rustling and moving in the trees towards the burn which I thought might be deer. The pike over the fire was getting all shrivelled and was black. It looked like a bin bag hanging on paracord. Far off I heard a fox bark which is not really like a bark, it is like someone with a husky voice shouting 'ack'. I am not scared of the dark or being outside at night. I like it. I needed to just sit and watch the fire to make me feel more calm about Peppa. I was thinking about what to do if she stayed poorly. I could go into the town and get a doctor but that would be it and we'd be found and I'd get arrested. I could go into the town and try to get more antibiotics and bandages and look up stuff on YouTube and websites about infections. But either way I'd have to leave Peppa. I also knew I'd have to go and snare something or catch more fish or shoot birds or our food would run out again.

I went into another kind of dream staring at the fire and saw the little lights and felt the tapping feeling at the base of my neck and I couldn't feel my body again and felt like I was peering out of a big black space at the fire and I stayed like that for ages.

The sun started to come up and the sky in the east through the trees got a thin strip of gold along the horizon and then it went bright pink and then silver and the frost sparkled all around the wood.

Then I heard rustling and feet stamping along from up above us, twigs were cracking and I felt my heart start racing. She appeared from round the back of the bender and she peered in under the umbrella at me sitting by the fire and said 'Guten Morgen Kinder.'

She did look like a witch and she had a big tartan shawl wrapped around her head like an African woman and her coat was long and black. She had scarves and bits of bright silk round her neck and she was wearing sheepskin gloves and carrying a walking stick. Just below her eye the scar was like a wee bit of white spaghetti stuck to her cheek. She smiled and she had big white teeth and her lips were red with lipstick.

I said 'Is it true you're a doctor? Peppa's ill. She got
bitten by a pike and it's got infected and she's had fever and
diarrhoea.'

She looked into the bender and went 'Ach so. The little
girl with red hair? And you are the sister.'

And I said aye and then she said 'I am a doctor. I am
an immunologist and I specialise in diseases of the immune
system. I was trained in the German Democratic Republic,
the DDR – do you know this?'

I said 'Can you make her better?'

And she said yes.

She went into the bender and crouched down next to
Peppa who started to wake up and when she saw Ingrid
said 'Hello Ingrid. I got bit by a pike.'

Ingrid smiled and pulled off her gloves and stroked
Peppa's head and said 'I am going to treat you.' Ingrid's hands
were big and she had long nails with red nail polish on
them. And her hands were really clean too.

She turned to me and said 'Tell me about the treatment
so far please.'

And I told her about washing the cuts and the Amoxicillin
and the painkillers and making Peppa drink a lot and the
pine needle tea. I told her the cuts kept oozing and bleeding
and about the red lines up Peppa's arm. And she listened
and kept going 'Gut . . . gut . . . gut' and then she said
'Excellent, you are a very intelligent young person.'

Then she said 'Boil water please and please hand me the
headlight.' And she started undoing the bandage with her
big hands and put on the head torch over her big tartan
thing and switched it on. I got the kettle going again and
poured her a cup of hot almost boiling water. She got it
and emptied it over her hands and rubbed them together.
It must've burned but she didn't look bothered. Then she

shook her hands till they were nearly dry and there was steam coming off them. She opened up the bandage and looked at all the cuts and all the swelling. She ran her finger along one cut and Peppa went 'Ow!' and then she pressed on the swollen bit and then she sniffed the cut.

Then she looked into Peppa's eyes very hard with the lamp, then she felt all round the back of Peppa's head and then under her neck and chin. Then she said 'Put the arms up' to Peppa and Peppa held her arms up like a diver. Ingrid felt all in under her armpits. Then she pulled back the sleeping bag and blanket and felt all down and around the tops of Peppa's legs and around her belly. While she was doing this I was watching and Peppa looked at me and grinned and held her eyes wide open and mouthed 'Lezza!' and pointed at Ingrid, and I laughed.

Ingrid made Peppa lie back down and covered her but kept her left arm out over the covers. Then she turned around and said 'The wound is getting further infected from foreign bodies that are still in it, which is why it has not begun to heal or form a scab and is still creating pus. It is also why she is feverish as her immune system is starting to react as if she has sepsis. The red track marks are immune responses to the foreign infection source.'

I said 'I cleaned it all with iodine.'

Ingrid said 'If there was further infection sources in the wound itself it would have made no difference. So. Do you know what sphagnum moss is?'

I nodded and Ingrid told me to go and get a big armful of it and wash any dirt or leaves off in the burn. I ran down to a flat bit just along the burn where the trees are thinner and there is a thick bed of moss growing alongside the water. I peeled a big slab of it up and it cracked where there was frost on the top. It was heavy and drippy and I squeezed it to get it drier then I washed it in the fast bit of the burn. My hands were icy and red while I washed it and I squeezed the water out and made sure there was no bits or twigs or dirt. Then I ran back and Ingrid was by the fire and she had a little zipper case in front of her. She was holding long tweezers in the flame of the fire. She let the ends glow red and then she laid them on a rock.

When she saw the moss she said 'Gut' and then said 'Do you have a cord?' I got her the roll of paracord and she took off a scarf from round her neck that was off white and looked like silk. She spread it out on the rock and then put all the moss into the middle of it and then tied the corners up into a kind of bag. She got out a folding knife and cut a length of paracord and then tied up the bag round the knot and made a loop in the top. Then she hung the bag over the fire from the umbrella and then put the kettle under it sitting so the spout was under the bag. The kettle soon started boiling and the steam was pumping out and up into the bag of moss. Ingrid hung the tweezers off the paracord bit so they were in the steam too.

'Make sterile' she said.

I sat on a rock on the other side of the fire and watched the steam billowing around the bag of moss.

I said 'What's in her cut?'

She said 'If I guess I will say teeth.'

'Teeth?'

'Pike teeth. They are quite fragile and thin and they snap off in prey. I have treated a pike bite before many years ago on a fisherman in Germany. Do you have a mother?'

I said 'Aye.' But I didn't want to tell her anything about us.

She was looking at me and she smiled again. 'You are very tall and very beautiful' she said. 'Is your mother here?'

I said 'No. We're on our own. I look after Peppa. We've been hunting and snaring rabbits and fishing for food.'

Ingrid smiled again. When she smiled her eyes went thin and even more Chinese and all round her eyes wrinkled up into little ridges. Her skin looked like it was all covered in tiny little cuts and it was the same colour as her silk scarf. She wore really red lipstick and she had dark eye shadow and mascara.

She said 'I live in a bender. Mine is bigger than this. I also have a drying rack for wood and a food store.'

'Where is it?' I said.

'About five kilometres over . . .' She pointed north towards Magna Bra. 'On the other side of the stones in a little valley with a stream.'

'How long have you lived there?'

'I have been here for four years. And before I was further down my valley nearer to the town and the main road. But I don't like to see people too much.'

Then I wanted to tell her about us and Robert and the police and the social after us. And see if she said she'd tell, but Peppa shouted 'I need a wee!' from the bender, and I went and got her and walked her over to the latrine.

When we got back Ingrid asked if we had soap and I got it from the backpack and she poured a tiny bit of boiling water onto her hands and then washed them with the soap and kept rubbing and rubbing and holding them over the steam. Then she shook them again in the heat off the fire. She said 'Please can you give two of the painkillers now. And Peppa sit on the bed.' I got two ibuprofen and codeine and gave them to Peppa who swallowed them and made a face. She sat on the bed with her arm out on her lap. Ingrid took the bag of moss and opened it and it was steaming and she got the tweezers and wiped them on the silk.

Wearing the head torch she knelt in front of Peppa and said 'So . . . this will sting you' and I held Peppa's other hand. First Ingrid squeezed some of the moss a bit drier and then laid it all over the cuts. It was still steaming and Peppa just said 'Hot' but she didn't flinch. Ingrid made sure it was all over the cuts and then she said 'We wait.'

We sat there and then Peppa said 'You can't tell anyone we're here Ingrid.'

Ingrid said 'Who is looking for you?'

I said 'Peppa don't say . . .' but Peppa said 'The police and social workers. We ran away. If they catch us they'll split us up and Sal will get put in the jail.'

Ingrid sat back. She closed her eyes and said 'I will never inform on anyone. When I was young I lived in DDR and there were informants everywhere who told the authorities everything they wanted to know about you. I had very good friends, I thought good friends, who told the government about things I had said or people I had been with or places I wanted to go. And my life was made very bad for a time. One informer was a man who I loved. I do not trust anyone who informs Peppa.'

Peppa said 'What's DDR?'

I said 'Is it in Germany?'

Ingrid opened her eyes and held her finger up. She leant forward and pulled all the moss off Peppa's hand and wrist. She threw it back out of the door of the bender. The cuts were really clean with no pus or blood and the edges were white. Peppa's skin looked whiter where the moss had been. Ingrid bent forwards with the tweezers and put the torchlight onto the cuts and said 'Hold' and I held Peppa's hand and she squeezed her eyes shut and so did I.

I felt Peppa flinch once and Ingrid go 'Ach so. Gut. Einer. Ah. So. Und noch einer. Und. Noch einer. So.'

I opened my eyes and so did Peppa and Ingrid said 'Good. Look.' And she held out her hand with the light on it and there were three little triangle shapes that looked like they were made of plastic. They had sharp edges on two sides and a thicker edge on the other. I said 'Are they pike teeth?' and Ingrid said 'They are. And now they are out and so the infection will go.'

Peppa looked at them for ages and then said 'What a bastard he was.'

Ingrid laid more moss on the wound and then bandaged it. She made Peppa wriggle her fingers and then she put her hand on Peppa's head and said 'Now you will be okay pretty girl.'

I knew that I liked Ingrid then and I thought I could maybe even tell her about killing Robert. I made tea and I got the cake out and we had belVitas and nuts and raisins. Ingrid asked about how much food we had and if we filtered the water. I told her we boiled it and we had corned beef and some beans and belVitas and cake and some raisins and nuts and a bit of bread. I said I was going to check the snares and she said 'Rabbit is good meat. But now I go. I will go to the stones and then to my bender. I will return tomorrow. You must give the last two antibiotics now and Peppa rest and drink fluids.'

She stood and pulled on her gloves and got her stick. Peppa said 'Thank you Ingrid. You're nice. Will you teach me to speak German tomorrow?'

And I said 'Yes, you are nice.'

Ingrid smiled at us both and said 'And you are both nice. And tomorrow I will teach you German and bring you some dried mushrooms.' And then she went striding off into the woods.

Peppa rested and slept and I went out and checked the

snares and we'd got a rabbit and I felt brilliant that Peppa was going to be better and we had a rabbit for our tea. It was sunny and cold on the big slope down to the loch and I thought about Ingrid and thought it was good for us we had met her because she wouldn't tell and she was a doctor. I wanted to know about DDR too so I was going to ask her a lot of questions when she came back.

Chapter Nine

Mushrooms

The next day Peppa was better and she got up and went running around the forest for an hour in the morning. I changed the bandage on her arm the night before and the swelling was going down and I put more moss on and bandaged it up again.

When Peppa got back we went to the burn and washed socks and knickers and I washed the bandages. Then we boiled the kettle and we both washed again with soap and a wet T-shirt for a flannel. It was still cold but I got the fire going well and even nude it was okay by the fire, and Peppa went on about pubes again.

We hung all the washing over the umbrella to dry and then I went out with the airgun over the warrens and sat still by the rocks and watched for rabbits. Peppa stayed in the bender reading *Kidnapped* which she said was slow and had a lot of old-fashioned words in it, but it was about a boy whose uncle was trying to kill him for an inheritance so far as she had got. And the old man uncle only ate porridge and he called it 'parritch'.

I stayed as still as I could and the wind was coming

northeast but only a little breeze along the loch and my scent would be away from the rabbits. I pumped the gun eight times and put a pellet in and lined up the sight on some ferns next to where I could see a run. And waited.

The ground under my bum was damp and cold. I leant against the rock with the gun propped along it. In front of me I could see the bracken and grassy slope with the trees behind. The sun was out but it was cold and my hands started feeling smooth like they do in cold wind.

I sat and watched the grass and ferns where the warrens were. Nothing moved apart from the ferns waving in the breeze. Further down three crows were flying around and around at the edge where the trees started. At the bottom the loch glinted in the sun. Above me the slope ran up and there were more trees, big Scots pines and larch, and above them you could see the top of the rocky ridge and over that was the moor and Magna Bra. It was nice knowing where I was and knowing Peppa was in the shelter reading.

I heard the rumble of a car before I saw it. Then two 4x4s came along the edge of the loch on our side. One was a green ranger's truck and the other was polis with an orange and yellow strip down the side. They were going slow driving along the loch shore where it was flat and stony.

I froze and watched, pulling back from the edge of the rock so I could just see them with one eye peeping round. I breathed slow and knew not to make any sudden emotional decision but to stop and pause and assess the situation.

The two trucks came slowly along almost to the beach where Peppa and I fished and stopped. The polis one pulled up onto the bank and two coppers got out. A ranger in a dark green shirt got out of the other truck and they walked up the slope a bit and stopped. The ranger was pointing and the coppers were both looking at phones. I could see one copper showing the ranger a phone and then he pointed the other way over towards the far side of the loch and they turned and looked across.

I turned round really slowly to see if there was any smoke coming up out of our woods from our fire. There wasn't and I knew most of it was being blown away off into the woods behind us in the breeze and there wouldn't be much anyway because we had really dry wood. I turned back slow and got by the edge of the rock and watched again.

They were all standing by the polis car now and talking and one was still looking at his phone. I waited and watched and breathed slow. Then the two coppers got back in their truck and the ranger got in his and they started again going along the loch towards the end. I waited till they were out of my sight and I couldn't hear the rumble of their engines. I guessed they would go to the far side and then try to get up the bank alongside the other burn and up towards the plantations and the forestry road we used.

If they were looking for us they weren't looking very hard, I thought. They didn't drive up towards our woods. Maybe they weren't looking for us. But two coppers. And a ranger. And they had the CCTV from the station and maybe even from on the train so they'd know which direction we went in.

I got up and crept back along and into the trees and then ran all the way back to our bender.

Ingrid was there when I got back and she had brought a Tupperware box full of dried mushrooms and another with butter in it, and bread and a frying pan.

Peppa said 'Did ye get a rabbit Sal?'

I said 'No' and then I said 'There's coppers down by the loch with a ranger in four by fours.'

Peppa said 'Shit. Shit. Shit. Shit.'

Ingrid said 'They look for you?'

'I don't know but why would they be up here?'

'Maybe they find a crime here' said Ingrid.

Peppa said 'Did they see you?'

'No. They went along the loch all the way up to the end. They stopped at our fishing place and got out and looked about.'

Peppa said 'We should move Sal. Go further up, go further into the woods at the top.'

Ingrid said 'Come to my camp. I am a long way from here and it is a little valley and I see nobody. I can make a bender for you. You bring your tarp.'

I needed to think so I wandered off into the wood for a bit. If they had come this near they might come further, they might even try to make it up to the other side of our wood and then if they came in they might find trails we'd left.

I went back and Ingrid was frying the mushrooms in butter and they smelled lovely. She got a tin of our corned beef and broke it all up into the pan with the mushrooms and fried it all.

Peppa said 'Let's go to Ingrid's bit Sal. It's further away and there's nobody there. We can make a new bender.'

'And you can get wood for me' Ingrid said. 'I am old and my back hurts sometimes.'

I said 'Don't you want to be on your own?'

Ingrid said 'No. I am on my own for many, many years. I would like to have two girls there.'

We ate the corned beef and mushrooms out of the pan and it was really nice and Peppa danced about going 'Nice food Ingrid!'

Ingrid didn't want to know why the polis were after us

or why we didn't want to see anyone else. I think that was why I decided we should go and stay at her bender. Maybe only for a bit and then come back this way. I could snare and hunt over there for all of us.

I said 'Is there a loch for fishing by you?'

She said 'Away up, above me and over. It is about two kilometres from my camp. A small loch. It is called Loch of Dudgeon. There is also a river at the bottom of my valley and I have a burn just next to me for water.'

'What if we get seen going there, over the moor and Magna Bra?'

'You have head torches – we go at night!'

I thought about it again and Peppa said 'Let's go Sal. We can go tonight.'

I said 'It's a long way Peppa. And we have to carry all the stuff.'

She said 'I know.'

I got my map out of the rucksack and worked out where Ingrid was. It was still far from houses or tracks but only about two miles from a main road. There were no tracks or footpaths marked leading to the little valley from the road and it all looked like dense woods between her and the road. I showed her the map and she showed me about where she was. The loch was at the top of her valley in the high ground where it rose up and led to Magna Bra one way and then onto moor and a chain of small lochs the other way.

I said 'Can we get food there?'

Ingrid said 'I have food. Much food. I go to the town once a month. I walk and get rice and flour and butter and jam. I can make bread. I have a stone bread oven.'

Peppa said 'Jam Sal!'

So I said okay, and Ingrid said we should go once it got

dark but we needed to pack up and clear all the bender and not leave any traces that we'd been there. So Peppa and I packed everything in the rucksack and I pulled all the branches off the bender and got the tarp down and pulled the umbrella apart and hid all the branches off in the wood.

We hid all the spruce in the bushes and pulled all the poles down from the bender. I zipped all our wet stuff into a pocket in the rucksack and we buried all the rubbish like cans and plastic bags. Peppa packed her stuff into the backpack and took her books and the pile of rabbit fur she'd tried to make a hat out of.

We sat round the fire until it started to get dark and I left the solar charger out in a patch of sun by the burn to charge the batteries for the head torches.

There wasn't any moon, and after it got dark we put the fire out with dirt and then kicked the ashes all over to hide where it was. There was nothing left of our camp when we started off up through the woods along the burn, only some bent twigs and flattened bits of grass.

Ingrid went in front with a head torch and Peppa went in the middle with the other one and I came behind and followed Peppa's light. Ingrid walked quite slow and she jigged up and down when she walked and she chattered to herself in German.

It was slow and hard going up through our woods and then we had to climb the big slope up to the moor at the top. Ingrid just kept going slow. Sometimes she looked back at us and went 'Come!'

When we got onto the moor we stopped and I put the rucksack down and Peppa sat on her backpack. Ingrid gave us water from her water bottle and we ate some belVitas.

It was darker than black on the moor. When we switched off the head torches the sky was huge over us and all pricked with stars and the more you stared the more you could see lines and swirls of them. In the middle it swirled away like water down a plug with all the stars getting tinier and tinier and fainter and fainter in a curling cloud. There were too many. Too many stars and planets in every direction and it made me feel swirly-headed looking at them. Ingrid stood looking up and held her hands up above her head and said 'It is the thing we will never know.'

I got the same feeling when I saw pictures of big crowds in Russia or China or Malaysia or Brazil on the internet and you saw how big cities were and how many people there were in the world. Or the feeling on a bus looking at people's houses going by and thinking there were all those people in the world and you would never know them or speak to them or even see them and they would never know you. It's a funny feeling like being scared and happy at the same time.

Ingrid didn't seem to need a compass and she just went straight out across the moor and our feet made a swishing sound going over the heather. In some places it was haggy and there were wee troughs full of wet peat and in some places we squelched over sphagnum moss. Peppa kept going well and it was me who was puffing following her and the round beam from her head torch dancing on the heather or on Ingrid's back.

The ground was starting to rise more as we went on and soon we were climbing again and Ingrid said 'We go through the stones . . .' A bit further on we stopped again. We were on a flat and in the torch beam you could see the stones poking up out of the heather. Peppa spun round and lit up the whole circle of them, most were shorter than me and some were long and lying on their sides. They were different shapes, some with pointy tops and some were round or like triangles and they were all silver grey and gold with lichen patches. We rested right in the middle of them and I got Peppa's head torch and counted twenty-four going right round us. It was silent and the dark was pushing in from the sky.

Ingrid stood right in the middle with her hands held up and she was talking to herself again in German with her eyes closed. Then she said 'I ask for blessing on us and keep us safe.'

Peppa was giggling and when I shone the head torch on her she was making the loony sign with her finger by her temple. I said 'Don't Peppa.'

Ingrid shouted 'Come' and we went on following her away from the stones and right across the moor top where the ground was mostly flat but slightly going down and we had the swish of us on the heather again.

We stopped three more times for water and belVitas and a rest. We'd been going hours and I was wondering where we were and thought I'd get the map out when I heard Ingrid say 'Here are my woods.'

And we plunged into a thick wood on a tiny thin path between the trees. It was more oak and hazel and alder than our woods. It was lower too, we'd dropped a good bit since the moor top and the stone circle. Ingrid kept on slow and steady and kept calling back 'Not far now little girls' and started going down a steep bank on the path which was a deer path because I could see tracks in the mud. We dropped and dropped and then we were on a flat bit that ran along the river and you could hear the water bubbling and swishing through the trees. Peppa complained her trainers were rubbing and I had to stop and get the first aid kit out of the rucksack and put a fabric plaster over her heel. The wood was lovely and quiet with just the sound of the little river and the breeze in the trees.

We climbed up again through the trees on another deer path and then we came to a kind of step sticking out over the bank and Ingrid said 'My camp!'

Her bender was along away from the edge and it was bigger than ours with an arch door and a green cloth hanging down over it. Next to it was a big drying rack made of logs stacked with wood. It had a roof made from spruce branches and then next to that was a stone dome made of rocks like a drystane dyke. In front of the bender was a fireplace made from rocks with a tripod over it and a big black kettle hanging and over the fireplace was a shelter like mine thatched with spruce. It was a good camp.

Peppa ran round looking at everything and shouted 'Sal!' and went over past the bender and there was a little burn running out of the rocks above making a waterfall into a wee pool. Behind the camp the slope went up with big rocks and birch and rowan trees growing out of it and clumps of dying bluebell leaves and brambles all twined in amongst the rocks.

Ingrid was lighting the fire and she called 'Do you like it?' and Peppa said 'It's brilliant. Can you swim in the wee pool?'

Ingrid said 'I wash in it and use it for water and I wash clothes in it. In summer you can sit in it to stay cool.'

I got my compass out and sat by Ingrid's fire. The camp faced south, good for sun and shelter from a north wind. I couldn't wait for morning so I could see the view down from it into the wood towards the river which you could still hear tinkling rushing. Nobody would find you here.

Peppa sat by the fire which was going now and felt lovely and lit up the camp around us and Ingrid said 'I have bread and cheese' and went into her bender.

Peppa said 'They won't find us here Sal.'

I said 'No. We'll need to see what it's like round here

in the morning. But it's better than where we were. Not so close to tracks or roads.'

Peppa said 'Ingrid's mad.'

I said 'I know. But she's nice and she likes us.'

Ingrid came back with three plates and big hunks of bread and butter and big pieces of cheese and a jar of pickle. She said 'Eat' and we did. I was really hungry and the bread was lovely and soft and tasted of smoke. The cheese was sharp and salty and it was lovely with pickle on it. We didn't talk for ages and Peppa ate everything really quick and Ingrid said 'Do you like an apple?' and Peppa said 'Aye.'

Then Ingrid said 'You sleep in my bender and I sleep here by the fire to watch.' And she jumped up and went into the bender and dragged out a big rush mat and a sleeping bag and a blanket. She laid the mat out along by the fire and got into the sleeping bag and pulled the blanket over her and sat up and said 'Warm here.'

Peppa said 'Ingrid how did you find us? How did you find where we were?'

And Ingrid said 'I smelled your fire. I can smell very well. I was up on the moor on my walk and I smelled your fire. And I knew it was going out and getting low so I came to look. And I saw you little girl asleep and the fire going out.'

I'd been wondering that too. Ingrid pointed to her nose. 'I can smell things a long way. I can smell if dogs are near and I can smell cars and sometimes people coming if the wind is right. I can smell rain coming and snow. I have a very good nose.'

Peppa said 'You wouldn't want to smell one of Sal's farts' and Ingrid said 'I don't mind farts. We all fart. I fart a lot.'

'So does Sal' Peppa said.

I said 'Did you smell the polis car today?' and she said 'No. Wind was wrong way. Now I need to sleep.'

She lay down in her sleeping bag and we banked up wood on the fire for her and then went into her bender.

She had a platform bed like ours with spruce branches on it. On some big flat rocks she had blankets and quilts and eiderdowns all neatly folded up and there were plastic boxes with lids on. She had a hanging rail made of stripped poles and on it were clothes and jackets and dresses all hanging off hangers like in a wardrobe. One was a Chinese silk jacket with dragons and fir trees and fish all embroidered on it in red and gold thread. She also had loads of pairs of boots all lined up round the edge of the bender, some were long riding boots, there were Dr Martens, long blue leather lace-up boots, walking boots, Converse boots and two pairs of big army boots.

Peppa said 'She likes her boots.'

We got out our sleeping bags and blankets and slept on the bed and it was warm and comfortable. I was so tired I couldn't stay awake to tell Peppa stuff and she was asleep quick too.

Chapter Ten

Camp

Things were good with Ingrid. We had food and I hunted in the woods. There were pheasants in her woods which means there was a shoot somewhere because pheasants are not native to Scotland and are introduced so rich people can pay farmers to shoot them. And they are really easy to shoot. They make loads of noise and they can't stay in camouflage and they sometimes just sit there while you line up the sight on them. Anyone can hit a pheasant. I could probably have got one with the slingshot. I got two on the first day we were at Ingrid's bit.

Peppa and Ingrid stayed in the camp and washed some clothes and hung them to dry and then Ingrid started trying to make the rabbit skins Peppa had sewn into a proper hat for her. It was getting colder but the sun was out in the day and it was frosty at night. Peppa read her book and Ingrid sat by the fire and cut the skins up and measured bits of them round Peppa's head and then started sewing them. While she was doing this she started teaching Peppa German words and first she had to teach Peppa all the German swear words. She didn't mind and even though she was old she thought it was normal to teach Peppa how to say fuck and wanker and arsehole in German. She said 'These are the most interesting words in a language. They are not bad words they are just words.' And Peppa asked her how to say bollocks and balls and cock.

When I got back with the Pheasants Peppa told me that 'Popantz' is the German for bogey and bra in German is 'Büstenhalter' which means bust holder and cock was 'Schwanz'. I plucked the pheasants and Ingrid said to keep the long tail feathers to make decorations but she called them 'decoratives'.

I gutted them and then we put salt on them and roasted them over the fire on sticks. Ingrid cooked rice in the big kettle and we had rice and roast pheasant. Afterwards Ingrid got apples from a box she kept them in all wrapped in tissue paper and they were red and sweet.

Ingrid said 'Tomorrow we make you a bender. I need my bender soon because it will snow in perhaps two days' time.'

The next day we got up early in the frost and I went off and cut saplings for our bender. We built it just up from Ingrid's so the doorway was close to the fire. I used rocks to make three plinths and then cut more poles to make our bed. I had to climb up above the camp to find spruce and while I was doing that Ingrid and Peppa started lashing the saplings together with paracord.

I had to go right up into the woods where I could see the dark green tops of spruce and I found about eight big ones amongst the other trees. I cut bundles of branches and lashed them together with two ends of paracord and then used it as a handle to drag them back down. We tied the tarp over the top of the frame and then wedged the spruce boughs over it in layers from the top down. I had to go and get branches twice more because we thatched it right to the ground and then put rocks on the ends of the branches on the ground to keep them down and make it windproof. We made a nice big arched doorway and I could almost stand up inside the new bender. Then Ingrid got us to pile dry leaves all around the outside walls and pile leaves on top for more insulation. It smelled lovely inside of spruce and dry leaves and we put spruce branches on the bed and all over the floor for a carpet.

Ingrid made candles out of birch bark rolled tight and pine resin she got from Scots pine trees. She also made waterproof bowls and a jug from birch bark with pine resin melted on the joints to make them watertight. She had a big tin of the resin she tapped from the trees and she warmed it up and showed us how well it burned. She said you could use it for glue and sticking wood together and it was also an antiseptic, an anti-inflammatory and it kills bacteria in wounds so you could use it to make dressings.

We made bread with the flour and dried yeast and salt and butter and kneaded it all in a big metal bowl Ingrid had. She showed us what to do and how to leave it for an hour by the fire to rise. Then we kneaded it again with more flour and Ingrid made a big flat ball of the dough and we put it on a flat rock and waited another hour. Ingrid lit her oven. It was a big dome made from rocks all put together in a circle and it had a thick flat rock on the top. There was a little doorway and Ingrid lit sticks and dry grass inside from an ember and when it was going she piled in wood and sticks and it smoked and blazed inside. There was a big flat rock on the floor and when the fire had burned down and was charcoal and hot embers she brushed all the ash to the sides and scooped up the dough on a slate and then pushed it over onto the flat rock.

The bread was brown and gold when it came out and me and Peppa ate it while it was still hot and Ingrid melted cheese on hers and had cheese on toast.

Just when Ingrid said it would, it started snowing and that night we all sat by the fire with blankets round us while the snow came down and the fire made it look yellow and orange. We had bread and cheese and tea with sugar but no milk. Peppa told us the story of *Kidnapped* so far.

The boy was called Davy and the story happened in 1751 and his uncle didn't want him to inherit his big house after his father had died even though he was the one who should've got it. So the uncle tried to kill him first by tricking him into climbing a big stone staircase with stairs missing over a big drop onto rock in the pitch dark. He was only saved by lightning when he saw where the missing stairs were and realised his uncle was trying to kill him.

Then the uncle got him to go to Edinburgh to see a lawyer but tricked him into getting on a boat and paid the captain to knock Davy out and kidnap him and take him to America where he would be a slave. I said I thought only black people from Africa got taken to America to be slaves but Peppa said it said in the book that Scottish people got sent too. So that's something I learned.

Anyway, on the ship the captain and the mate and the other bloke are drunk all the time and torture a boy called Ransom to death and Davy has to go and serve them food and brandy. And then they go into fog and they run down a small boat, and on the boat is a Highland man called Alan Breck Stewart who says he is a king and is carrying loads of money for his chief and he speaks in Scots words. The captain, who is bad even though Davy thought he was good when he met him in Edinburgh, and the other men who drink all the time, plan to kill Alan and take all his money and Davy overhears them making a plot and so he makes friends with Alan and they have a big fight in a place called the roundhouse on the ship and Davy kills a sailor with a gun and they stab Mr Shaun who was the one who killed the boy and he dies too.

And then Peppa said 'What's a whig?'

Ingrid said 'Hair, for your head if your own hair falls out.'

And Peppa said 'No. It's W-H-I-G. What is it Sal?'

But I didn't know and I wished I had Wikipedia. Peppa said 'Anyway, Alan Stewart said whigs have got long faces.' And Ingrid and me looked at each other and we both frowned and shrugged.

I said to Peppa 'How old is Davy?' and Peppa said she thought he was thirteen or fourteen.

And I said 'He killed someone.' And Peppa said 'Aye' and he did, defending Alan in the roundhouse.

Peppa learned loads of German words from Ingrid while I was out setting snares or trying to shoot pheasant. I went down to the river and set two night lines with worms on the hooks on them for eels. I found another warren along from the camp in a clearing where there was a bank and there were rabbit tracks in the snow. I set some snares in the runs there.

When I got back to the camp Peppa had learned German words for bits of her body and kept pointing at her elbow and going 'Ellbogen' or at her ear and going 'Ohr' and her eyes were called 'Augen'. Finger was 'Finger' and hand was 'Hand' with a T sound on the end. Then she pointed at her arse and went 'ARSCH'.

We collected all the wood we could too because the store was running low and Ingrid said pulling wood and snapping it all up made her back hurt and she was old.

The snow made the days really bright and it clung on the trees and bushes and at night the sky cleared and it froze. Ingrid finished Peppa's hat and Peppa wore it. It had flaps down over the ears and a peak and the fur was on the inside and she said it was cosy. Ingrid was good at sewing and making things and at night she carved shapes into wood with her knife while we sat by the fire.

One night after we'd had eels and rice I said 'Ingrid how old are you?'

And she smiled and said 'I am seventy-five years old.'

Then she told us about her life and how she got to the woods and was surviving.

She was born in Berlin in Germany in 1940 which was the second year of the Second World War and her father was in the German army and her mother was from Latvia which is near Russia and they had met when they were both servants in a big house for rich people before the war started. She said they lived in a little flat on the ground floor of a block of flats in a poor part of Berlin which was all full of Nazis and Nazi flags. Her dad was not a Nazi but he had to join the army anyway and when she was one he got killed when a plane full of German soldiers crashed going to Poland.

Her mum got money off the government then because her dad had been in the army when he died but it wasn't enough to buy food and pay their rent so her mum used to clean offices and big buildings. Ingrid spoke Latvian at home with her mum and she spoke German when she was out or at nursery school and at home she called her mum 'Māte' which is Latvian for mother and the German is 'Mutti'.

The British and Americans started bombing Berlin and her and her maw had to sit in underground train stations called the U-Bahn while they were bombing. At nursery school they had to sing songs about Hitler and Germany winning the war but they never knew that the Russians had already beaten the German army and were invading and coming to Berlin. There were big guns in the park near where she lived that fired at the bombers all night long and all doorways and windows in her street had sandbags in them.

In the U-Bahn one night Ingrid's mum met an old man who she made friends with and he became her boyfriend and he started coming and sleeping at their flat and he brought them food and sometimes he brought wine and brandy for her mum and he brought Ingrid a doll and ribbons for her hair. His wife was dead and his two sons had been killed fighting the Russians in Russia.

The bit they lived in was getting bombed and shelled every day and they had no food because all the shops were blown up and there was rubble and collapsed buildings everywhere. Ingrid and her mum stayed in their flat and her mum went out some days and got bread and rice if she could find it. There was no gas to cook or electricity and they made fires out of wood outside their back door in the yard to cook and keep warm. All the Nazis were running and hiding and trying to get away because the Russian soldiers were coming and they would kill them.

The old man who was Ingrid's mum's boyfriend stopped coming and bringing them food and they started to starve and so did lots of other people who lived near them. Ingrid's mum cried all the time and they just stayed in their flat all day and listened to the guns and bombs getting nearer.

Then the Russians came in tanks and big long lines of

soldiers and they went into every flat and house and raped the German women. Three Russian soldiers burst into their little flat and raped Ingrid's mum while Ingrid was hiding in a cupboard where her mum made her stay all the time once the Russians came. Ingrid's mum got depressed after that and she just stayed in bed all day and Ingrid had to go out and find food and water.

But the bombing and the explosions all stopped and the Russians took over the whole area where they lived and there were soldiers in all the flats and houses and a big tent in the middle of the street where loads of them stayed. Some of the Russian soldiers were nice and gave Ingrid bread and cigarettes for her mum. The whole of Berlin got bombed and all the houses and blocks of flats were blown up and there were piles and piles of rubble and stones everywhere and nothing worked and they had to get their water out of pipes in the street and carry it home in buckets.

The Russian soldiers told her that Hitler was dead and Russia had won the war and now Berlin was part of Russia and she was going to be Russian not German. Lots of the German men got taken away and sent to Russia to work in factories, even the old ones, and Ingrid and her mum had to go and work in lines of women moving stones and rocks and rubble out of all the bombed buildings and clearing up all the mess after the fighting had stopped. They got fed in kitchens in the street and had to queue to get bread and soup every day.

Ingrid's mum got a new boyfriend who was a Russian officer called Ilya, and he was as big as a giant and he had a beard and wore a big coat with a fur collar. He came to their flat and Ingrid had to stay in their kitchen while him and her mum were in bed together. But he was nice and he brought them food like sausages and chocolate and cake. And he brought Ingrid's mum vodka and sometimes they got drunk and Ingrid went out and played in the streets in all the bombed buildings.

There were lots of kids who played out then on the streets and in all the buildings that were bombed and being pulled down. They were all like Ingrid and didn't have dads. It was hot and it was summer and sometimes they found dead people in old buildings and sometimes they could smell them before they found them. There were old German tanks and wrecked cars everywhere.

One day five of them were playing in a back court of some flats where there were piles of stones and dust. They had chalk and they were playing houses and they'd chalked all the rooms on the floor and Ingrid was the baby and two older girls were the mum and dad and another boy was the wee brother. One girl was running over a pile of rubble and a bomb went off in it. There was a blast and Ingrid got thrown across the court like a wee doll and she couldn't see for the dust and smoke. Her cheek was bleeding and burning. All the other kids were dead.

Some Russian soldiers ran in and rescued her and took her to the camp and she got seen by a Russian doctor. He pulled a lump of metal about the size of a peanut out of her cheek and then he stitched it and she screamed.

Ingrid's mum got a job working for the Russian soldiers in their camp cooking and cleaning and she started being out all day and leaving Ingrid. And at night she started going out too with Ilya and she was drunk a lot or at work and Ingrid could do what she liked.

She sometimes stayed out in the streets with older kids who nicked stuff from shops or off the Russians from their camp. Ingrid was wee and she could climb into places through small holes and she looked really sweet and innocent and they used her as a lookout while they burgled and nicked.

One boy called Klausi who was about twelve liked Ingrid and started looking after her and giving her food. He stopped other kids from bullying her and he took her with them when they all went out burgling and nicking. Sometimes they got sweets from army stores or shops that had opened up, and sometimes they nicked cigarettes out of vans that were delivering stuff to the army camps.

Klausi didn't have any parents and he lived in a cellar with his brother who was called Johannes – and they all called him Hansi – and they were leaders of a gang of kids who all stayed out on the streets all the time, nicking and begging and causing trouble.

The other women in the block they lived in didn't like Ingrid's mum and they used to spit on her and call her a 'Rabenmutter' which means 'raven mother' in German because they think ravens don't look after their kids and leave them in danger.

As it got towards winter Ingrid had to collect wood and make fires in the flat to keep warm because there was no heating or gas and they still had to get water from a pipe in the street. Her mum was there less and less and when she was, she was drunk.

And then one day she didn't come back to the flat at all.

Ingrid waited in the flat for days on her own and her mum didn't come. She went and found Klausi and the other kids and told them her mum was missing and Klausi said she might have got murdered by the Russians because they raped German women and sometimes killed them. For two days Ingrid walked around Berlin with Klausi and Hansi looking for her mum. They went to all the camps where the Russians were and they asked the soldiers if they had seen her but the Russians couldn't speak German and most of them chased them away or shouted at them. Then one day she saw Ilya standing by an army truck and talking to some other soldiers and she ran up to him and asked if he knew where her mum was. And he laughed and the other soldiers laughed at her and he gave her a piece of chocolate and rubbed her head and walked off.

She stayed in the flat and Klausi and Hansi came and lived there too and they all slept in her mum's bed. There was no school or parents or anyone to tell them what to do and they stole food or begged it and scavenged wood in the bombsites. At night they told each other fairy stories in the big bed and Klausi cuddled Ingrid when they went to sleep.

One day some old men came to the flat and banged the door in. They were polis and they spoke German and they were finding orphans to take to an orphanage. Klausi and Hansi didn't want to go with them and Klausi said they were going to take them to Russia to work in mines and the old men grabbed them both and one grabbed Ingrid and they carried them out of the flat. Klausi and Hansi got taken away and put in a big lorry they had outside.

The man who had Ingrid carried her down the street and then walked and walked with her in his arms until they got to a big grey building next to a church and then he gave her to a priest and she had to sit in a big room with lots of other little kids. The priest and some other German women gave them bread and soup and then the priest said a load of prayers and they all got given a blanket and had to sleep on the floor.

The next day they all had to have a bath and they all waited in a line in their knickers and then they got put in a tin bath full of grey cold water and a fat woman washed them with soap. Then they dried them all with rough towels and gave them new clothes. The girls had little grey dresses and a grey jumper and a wool coat and black berets to wear. They all got new pants and socks and they were all given a school bag that was made of canvas.

Then Ingrid had to tell a big ugly old man in a uniform her name and where she lived and her mother and father's name. She told him her father had died in the war and her mother had got murdered by the Russians and the man put his hand on her cheek and smiled at her.

They got taken outside then in a long line and all got into a big bus. There were about seventy or eighty kids all wee and all wearing the grey coats and berets. The bus drove them out of Berlin past all the buildings that were blown up and lines of people waiting for food and past hundreds and hundreds of Russian soldiers and tanks and lorries and huge guns. They got into the countryside and Ingrid had never seen the countryside before. All the trees were bare and there were huge bomb craters everywhere and grey snow. The bus kept stopping and Russian soldiers got on and walked up and down and looked at all the children.

The orphanage was a huge old building that looked like a castle by a lake and there were Russian army men there in tents and burned-out German tanks and cars. They got taken into big dormitories with rows of beds and little tables and they had to go to bed because it was so cold.

The orphanage was run by old nuns who were angry all the time and shouted at them if they talked. They all had to go to Mass and pray every day in a big hall. There were Russian soldiers there too and they laughed at the nuns and smoked and talked in the Mass.

After a few weeks they started going to school in the

big hall every day. They did reading and writing in German and they learned about Russia and then one day a big man came in and started teaching them Russian as well and they had to learn a new alphabet and new words. The Masses stopped as well and they didn't have to go to church and the priests stopped coming in to talk to them.

And that was where Ingrid stayed until she was seventeen.

She liked it there and she had good friends and she helped look after the smaller kids. She was good at maths and she learned about science and chemistry. She learned Russian and she learned all about the Russian Revolution and there were pictures of Comrade Lenin and Marx and Engels in the main hall and a big painting of Russian soldiers liberating Berlin in the entrance hall. There was a picture of Comrade Stalin in the hall until she was thirteen, and then there was a picture of Comrade Khrushchev. At weekends she went cycling with two girls her age called Irene and Anna and they were in an organisation called the Young Pioneers who were fighting to build socialism in Germany.

Sometimes she went into Berlin to party meetings and it was all still bombed and there were huge gaps in all the streets where buildings had been. All the old buildings had bullet holes in the stone. In the street where she used to live there was a new library and a university being built right where her flat had been. She didn't think about her mum or what it was like when she was wee then. She forgot a lot of things because she was young and very pretty and she liked being German and building socialism which meant that all the money was shared and there was no poor people and no rich people and everybody had a nice flat and a job and children went to good schools and got looked after properly.

Ingrid told us all this while we were sitting by the fire in the snow and we listened but when Peppa started yawning and her eyes started drooping Ingrid said 'I tell you more tomorrow.'

I wanted to hear more about her and why she was living in the woods now. She had come all across Europe and she had seen her mum get raped and probably murdered and she was still nice and she still looked after us.

Chapter Eleven

Food

In the morning it was really cold and Peppa and me stayed in bed and snuggled and talked. Ingrid got the fire going and brought us porridge with jam in it in her birch bark bowls.

She said 'Soon we must go to the town and get food and carry it back. And I get letters from the Post Office.' I knew we'd have to go sooner or later but I was worried if we all went we'd get seen and people would ring the police and tell about us. But I wanted to know what the police knew about us and if Maw was still in the rehab too. So we talked about it and decided that if me and Peppa dressed like lads, and if we split up in the town so we weren't together, and then met up later when we'd done the shopping, we wouldn't get noticed.

Ingrid said 'They all know me in the town. I was the doctor there once. They all think I am mad. People ignore me because I am old and mad. I also have money in a bank and I can get it and we can buy nice food and I would like also to buy a binoculars for you Sal and a proper knife for Peppa.'

So we both said 'Aye alright.' It was two miles to the road and then four miles to the town from where you came out, and there was a bus stop by the garage and Little Chef where you came out on the road. We took the backpack and the rucksack for the food and Ingrid wore a big wide hat made of waxy cotton that looked like a cowboy hat. We pushed all Peppa's hair up under her rabbit hat and I wore the beanie and I look like a lad anyway. I made Peppa wear her Helly Hansen in case it snowed or rained.

It only took about an hour to get to the road going down through the woods, crossing the river on stepping stones and then climbing up again over a ridge all covered in woods. We used mostly deer paths and tracks and Ingrid knew the way. You came out right on the road, and it was a main one and just up from us was the garage and Little Chef.

We waited till nothing was coming along the road and then split up and Peppa and Ingrid stood one end of the bus stop and I stood the other. No one else was waiting. We sat apart on the bus too. People might think Peppa was a lad out with her mad granny and I was just a lad going into town. The bus was empty apart from us.

We all got off at the stop before the centre of town and I waited at the bus stop and Peppa and Ingrid walked in along the riverside and over the bridge that led to the main street. We were meeting back on the bridge in two hours. I waited for a bit then walked in looking for CCTV cameras on the lampposts but there weren't any. I went straight to the library and the old man who spoke to me before wasn't there and they ignored me when I paid and got an hour online.

The headlines were still about the search for us and stuff about the continuing investigation, but they had got less and less. A few days before there were ones that said 'Body in loch *NOT* connected to missing girls say police' about a woman found dead in a loch in Lanarkshire not being me or Peppa. There were some stories about sightings of us. One said we had been seen in London and one had a blurry CCTV picture from Manchester saying we had been seen there so that was good. I searched a lot of different names, including Robert, and there was a story about him having convictions for sexual offences against a child from when he was twenty-three and being on the Sex Offenders' Register. There was a story about an investigation in the social services over why they never knew anything about us or ever came round. I knew why. Because we never said or told and Maw was lucky nobody shopped her when she was drinking and not looking after us. And I was looking after Peppa and her.

On the Police Scotland website there was a full report of us missing and a newer picture with descriptions and the CCTV stills from Glasgow, but that was it.

There was loads on Twitter still. All the same people posting, Ian Leckie and Mhari, and then I found @AlisonatTheClub and it said 'Spoke to Claire she is doing well in the rehab.'

And then ones from Maw from the past ten days. My heart started fluttering and it wobbled when I started reading it. I didn't even know she did Twitter. One said 'Praying still for ma lassies. Sal and Peppa please contact me. I love you both.' And then one saying 'Three weeks sober. One day at a time. I can't believe it. Coping with this with no painkillers!' and then loads congratulating her including Ian Leckie going 'If you do the right thing then the right thing will happen Claire. Stay in there. Stick to the programme.'

In one yesterday she said 'Am breakin all the rools here

doin this but I need to keep letting them know I am here an I love them. Sober 24 days. God protect my babies.' Then one came up while I was looking at her feed. She was posting right then. It said 'Coming up four weeks no drink. It is a miracle. Now I need another one. God bring back my girls.'

I left the library and got a pasty and a can of Coke from Greggs and went and sat on the bench looking at the river. Then suddenly Peppa came up and sat next to me. She said 'Give us some money. I want to buy Ingrid a present.'

I said 'Peppa you're not meant to be with me. What if we get seen together or on CCTV.'

She said 'Give us some money then.'

I said 'Don't nick anything, if you get caught they'll know who you are. Go on, stop talking to me.'

I gave her twenty quid and she ran off into the town. I looked all up and down the main street and I couldn't see any CCTV but they would have it in shops. There weren't that many people about but the street was busy with cars and buses and it was cold and there was slushy snow on the pavements.

I was feeling alright apart from being a bit scared about getting seen with Peppa. Maw had stopped drinking by the look of it and she was getting looked after in the rehab and the polis were clueless about us.

Behind the main street there was a big car park and a Tesco and I went there and filled the rucksack up with the food we needed. I got flour and rice and pasta and salt, and a big tin of dried milk and oats for porridge and butter and cooking oil. Ingrid said we needed more soap and shampoo so I got them and I got string. I bought some steak for our tea when we got back and I bought apples and big baking potatoes. And then loads of cheese and tins of beans. Ingrid was going to get cake and sugar and we had loads of tea still.

After I'd packed it all in the rucksack I walked back up to the bridge and watched down the main street and I saw Ingrid striding across the road from the Post Office and going into a shop but I didn't see Peppa. I saw Ingrid come out of one shop and then go into the Co-op.

We all met up a bit later. I was standing on the bridge and I saw Ingrid and Peppa both walking up towards me. Then an old man who was walking a wee dog stopped and started talking to Ingrid. She stopped too and was smiling and talking to him like normal. Peppa crossed over and ignored Ingrid and walked on up towards me. She was carrying two plastic bags and drinking a can of Irn-Bru.

I walked on ahead towards the bus stop and kept looking back and saw Peppa coming along behind me. Then a bit further back I saw Ingrid coming on the other side of the road. I suppose it looked normal and we didn't look like we were all together but you don't know what people notice or feel like telling the polis.

At the bus stop we all ignored each other and there was an old man and his wife there waiting too. Peppa kept looking across and catching my eye and grinning at me and I shook my head at her and looked to see if the old man and his wife had seen, but they hadn't. Ingrid just stood at the end straight upright staring out along the road and ignoring everyone. She had Peppa's backpack on and it was bulging with stuff she'd bought.

By the time we were all together on the path up into Ingrid's woods it was starting to come dark and was getting really cold. Ingrid said 'I met an old patient of mine from a long time ago and he was asking me about how I was and where I lived. I told him I was living in London and I was here on holiday. I said nothing about us and living here. I was rather surprised that he was still alive because he was a diabetic.' And she smiled at us and seemed pleased.

I said 'I found out about Maw. She's got sober and stopped drinking in the rehab. She's still in there and she keeps asking God to keep us safe.'

Peppa said 'If she is better we can go and get her.'

We were climbing up a steep bit where the snow was undisturbed by animals or feet and it was crunchy. On some places the trees were so thick they were like a solid wall but Ingrid knew how to worm through them in the little spaces and we got to the top and started coming down into the valley where the river was. The trees were thinner here and bigger and the valley swept down in a long slope towards the river and there were wee evergreens in between the trees and next to one was a big mound with new earth all thrown out of a hole and old dry grass lying outside. I stopped by it and said 'Look. Badgers.'

Ingrid said we should come and watch them one day, sit downwind and see them coming out and feeding and playing. 'They love to play and run around. They make very good paths to follow.'

I decided we would come back and watch them. Badgers don't hibernate like hedgehogs do. They still go out feeding and digging worms and grubs up as long as the ground isn't too frozen.

It was a hard climb back up to Ingrid's bit with all the shopping and me and Ingrid had to keep stopping and breathing but Peppa ran the last bit right up to the top and the camp behind the trees.

We got the fire going and Ingrid lit her candles and I cooked the steaks on a grill over the fire and we had them with beans and then we had cake and tea. Then Peppa said

'Ingrid I bought you a present.' And she got three silk scarves out of her plastic bag and Ingrid just sat with her mouth open and then she hugged Peppa really hard and put the scarves on. Peppa said 'I got them in a charity shop' and she gave me all the change from her twenty quid. And she showed me a book and said 'I got a new book too, and a wee reading light that clips on the page so I can read in bed in the bender.'

Then Ingrid said 'And now I have gifts for you little girls.'

She had bought me a monocular which is like a small telescope that you can use for spotting animals and things quite a long way off. It was fantastic and it had a magnification of 10x40 and came in a canvas pouch with a wrist band. Ingrid said 'Better than binoculars for spotting and also I had no idea if your vision was a perfect 20/20 so I decided to get a monocular. It is German and they make all the best optical equipment. Very good for hunting and watching birds.'

Without even knowing it was happening I started crying. It just suddenly rose up in me and I was greetin for the first time since I was about eight. I don't know why I did and Peppa said 'Sal . . .' I didn't sob or shake or make any sound, the tears just started pouring out of my eyes and I felt a huge hard knot in my chest. Ingrid put her arm around me and Peppa held my hand. I think it was getting a present. I couldn't remember the last time I'd got one. And it was such a brilliant present, not chocolate or perfume or make-up or something stupid. It was a monocular which is one of the best things you can ever have if you are like me.

Then Ingrid gave Peppa a knife. It was an excellent survival knife with a serrated cutting edge and a self-sharpening webbing sheath like the Bear Grylls knife. Peppa didn't cry. She jumped up and went 'Yesssss!' and ran around with it waving it and stabbing things and I shouted her to be careful. She probably is old enough to have a knife and she would like cutting wood and carving things as long as she didn't cut her fingers off.

We both said thank you to Ingrid, and Ingrid said 'You are making my life very happy Sal and Peppa.'

After that Peppa went to bed to try to finish *Kidnapped* and then start her new book which was about a boy whose mum died. Ingrid said 'Help me Sal' and we went over to near her bender and we brought a big birch log to the fire. Ingrid got her knife and said 'Now I show you how to make with birch bark.'

She scored it right around and then peeled the bark back and it came off and under it was yellow and glistening and smelled sweet. Then she put a wee can with pine resin in it on the fire to heat it. When she had a piece of bark about the size of A4 printer paper, she made four cuts into the corners about six centimetres long going diagonal towards the middle. Then she folded the edges in on each other and put her hands around it and closed it in on itself so it made a bowl with neat square corners. She said 'Silver on the inside, see . . . to make waterproof. Birch bark is full of oil.'

She heated her knife in the fire and then spread resin on the joins and held them. She said 'You can stitch this sometimes, but in the cold it will go hard and stick.'

She put the bowl down, away from the fire. It had a nice flat bottom and the edges and top were all neat. It looked lovely and after a few minutes Ingrid got some water from the plastic bottle and poured it in. And it didn't drip.

She gave it to me and said 'Drink.'

Her hands were big and bony and she had long nails that she had painted red. All the skin was crinkly like scrunched-up tinfoil but they were soft like velvet.

I said 'Did you like your maw's boyfriends?'

She said 'No. But some of them gave me things to eat and we were very hungry. My mother suffered a lot in the war. It is not easy to be a mother.'

I said 'Were you a mother?'

She said 'No. I wanted to be a mother. But it was not easy. In DDR after the war there was no fertility treatment.'

Ingrid said she went to university in East Berlin which was part of the DDR, or the GDR as we called it in Britain. She started studying chemistry but then she went into training to become a doctor, because in the DDR there were more opportunities for women to be doctors than there had been before the war, with the Nazis.

At the university she met a young soldier called Max who she fell in love with. He was doing training in electronics and he was tall and blond and had huge blue eyes and big strong hands. They were both in the SED which was the party that ran their country and it meant they could get jobs and flats and houses. The government built a wall round their part of Berlin to stop people getting out into the West of Germany and the rest of Europe which was all run by the Americans who were enemies of socialism and the German people. Max did patrols along the wall to stop people escaping. The people who wanted to escape thought that life would be better in the American sector where people had more money, but there was more poor people and unemployment and drugs there.

Ingrid didn't worry about people escaping because she was so happy learning about being a doctor and she started to do research into illnesses to find how people got them and she learned a lot about the body's immune system which is the white blood cells we have that fight infections and viruses.

She was so clever that she discovered things about the immune system and helped to make drugs to fight off diseases and drugs to make the immune system work better. She started working in a medical research place and Max got a promotion in the army and was in charge of electronic listening machines that they had to try and hear what the Americans were doing in the West of Germany where they had soldiers ready for another war with Germany.

Ingrid said she was happy for a while being married and living in a flat in Berlin with Max. They wanted to have children but she couldn't get pregnant no matter how much they did sex. They had friends they liked and they went out with but it was difficult to get all the things you could get in the West of Germany like TVs and vacuum cleaners and nice cars. But she still felt that she was trying to make Germany a better place and have a country where all the people shared and looked after each other.

Max was unhappy they didn't have children and Ingrid couldn't get pregnant and soon he started cheating on her with other women. And he drank a lot too, mostly vodka they got from Russia. Sometimes he went away to Russia or other parts of Germany for weeks and Ingrid was on her own in the flat and just going to work every day and researching.

She changed her job and started working in a People's Medical Centre where they treated workers and ordinary people who were ill. She saw a lot of people who were sick with illnesses that were easy to cure if they had the medicine and things they needed but they didn't. She often had to complain to people from the party and to older men doctors that they didn't have the things they needed for making the workers better, and the hospitals were all run down and had dirty wards and cracked windows.

Because Max was away a lot and when he was home he got drunk, they argued and she started getting depressed. And she knew people who told her about how different it was in the West and she heard pop music on radio from the West of Berlin and everyone seemed to be having a good time there.

Then Max told her he had got another woman pregnant and he was going to leave her and live with the other woman and have children and she got really depressed and sometimes even thought about committing suicide.

The police in the GDR were called the Stasi and they watched people they thought were American spies and who they thought wanted to destroy socialism and they watched anyone who moaned or criticised the government or the high-up people in power and sometimes people who moaned or complained got arrested and put in prison. It was not a democracy like Britain where you can say that the prime minister is a wanker and you hate the Tories and not get in any trouble. In the GDR you had to say and do what the government said and not complain and moan about the country and all the things that were wrong. And you couldn't leave either unless you were with Stasi people who stopped you from talking to people they didn't like and stopped you from running away to live in another part of Germany or America.

One day some Stasi people came to Ingrid's flat and told her Max had been arrested because he was an American spy and had been sending secrets about the GDR to Americans in West Berlin. Ingrid didn't believe it and they asked her all about Max and she told them about the drinking and the other woman and they asked her if she could think of anyone else she knew who might be an American spy and she said no. And they said if you do and you tell us we'll get you a better flat and even a car.

During this time Ingrid learned English so she could read English medical books and journals about immunology and because she was a party member she got to go on a trip out of the GDR to London to a conference where doctors from all over the world met to talk about their ideas about the immune system. Three doctors from the GDR went to the meeting which was held in a big house in the middle of London. They got told that they were going to see the capitalist system and that there was crime and drugs and poverty everywhere and the workers were all suffering because they were not allowed to have a socialist country like the GDR. But when Ingrid got to London she loved it. There were lights and theatres and red buses and loads of people and expensive shops with beautiful clothes in them. She heard pop music and saw hippies with long hair and weird clothes and everything was colourful and exciting in London. They had Stasi men with them all the time to stop them running away and they had to show everything they brought back to the GDR with them in case they brought illegal things or pop records or expensive clothes. But she had no money to spend in London, she just liked all the colourfulness and she liked the hippies and the music she heard. She said people looked happy and it felt like they were free.

When they got back they got asked by the Stasi who they had spoken to and what they had said and Ingrid got asked to tell if the other doctors had spoken to people or had tried to buy expensive clothes or gold or pop records. She said no.

She stayed in the GDR for another ten years until she was thirty-nine. She worked for the People's Medical Centre and she did research about the immune system and she lived in a small flat. She was told that Max had got executed for being a spy and other people she knew got arrested including both the girls she used to go cycling with, Anna and Irene. Anna worked for the government radio station and Irene worked at a big power plant in the countryside and they got taken away and put in prison for being spies. Some of the people in the university got arrested too and Stasi men started following Ingrid back from the university. And all the time she was thinking about running away and going to London. It became her dream to go there and live and be free and not get arrested for doing nothing wrong.

Sometimes she walked around East Berlin at night and walked along bits of the wall and looked over and you could see apartment blocks and cranes and buildings on the other side. In the middle was all barbed wire and there were machines guns to shoot people who tried to escape. She still never really thought about when she was wee or the things that happened to her mum. But inside she was sad and angry and she got depressed a lot. She listened to the BBC at night even though it was illegal and she found out about lots of things going on in Britain like workers going on strike and punk rock music. In the GDR she couldn't really trust anyone because people informed on their friends to get better flats and cars. The Stasi still came to see her and asked her about people she knew but she would never tell on them and she just said she didn't know anything. But they followed her and when she got letters or parcels sent from the UK or America about immunology they had been opened and looked at by the Stasi.

Then she wrote a research paper about immunology and the way that blood cells identify harmful things they need to kill which she discovered using a microscope and doing lots of tests on rats. The paper made her quite famous and she was asked to come to London again to another conference.

It took ages for the Stasi and the government to give

her permission but in the end they did because she was making East Germany look good in the West and they wanted to show how good the medicine they had was. She had three Stasi men with her who pretended they were doctors and they stayed with her all the time.

In London they had a hotel in Kensington which was posh and really expensive and the Stasi men were all really excited about it and they got drunk in the bar and made Ingrid sit with them while they drank and laughed. They were being watched too by British spies and Ingrid knew that one of the barmen was a spy because he didn't know how to pour beer and he kept looking at her and catching her eye.

She was going to defect. That means she was going to find a policeman and say she didn't want to go back to the GDR and she wanted to stay in London. She told the Stasi men she had got her period and she was feeling ill, and they were all drunk and they didn't want to leave the bar so they let her go up to her room in the hotel. But she didn't go to her room. She walked all through the hotel and found a door at the back that went into a yard and then an alley and then came out on a main street with shops and lots of traffic. It was almost midnight and she walked and walked to make sure they weren't following her and then she went into a police station and said 'I am an East German doctor and I wish to defect.' She didn't have a passport because the Stasi men had it but she had some letters about the conference and she had her SED party membership card and she showed the police and they made her sit in a room for two hours and made lots of phone calls. Then two men in suits came and took her away to a big office block in London and sat in a room with her giving her coffee and cigarettes and they waited until morning.

I went to bed after Ingrid had finished and she said she'd tell me more tomorrow but she was tired and she wanted to go to Magna Bra in the morning to talk to the Goddess. And I said okay.

I got into bed and Peppa was still awake and she was reading *Kidnapped* with her wee clippy light and I said 'Is it good?'

She said 'Well, I dinnae understand a lot of it because it's old-fashioned, but they get shipwrecked and then Davy gets washed up and stuck on an island and can't get across to the mainland because he doesn't know about tides and he thinks the sea will just stay the same all the time. Then he realises and he escapes and then he goes to find Alan. He has got a button off his coat so everyone knows he is Alan's friend because there are soldiers wanting to catch Alan. I'm not sure why. And then this bad man called the Red Fox gets shot when Davy is talking to him, and he has been stealing money off all the Highlanders in Appin where Alan is a chief of a clan. Davy runs to see who has shot him and he gets pulled into a bush by Alan who is watching him and the Red Fox up a hill . . . Oh, and Alan said he was going to kill the Red Fox so Davy thinks he did, but Alan said he didn't and then they get chased by soldiers all over the moors and heather and they have to sleep out. Oh, and they get stuck up on a rock in a glen and they can't get off or all the soldiers will see them and they only have brandy to drink and they need water and it is really hot. Does it get hot in the Highlands?'

I said 'Aye. In the summer. But it rains mostly.'

'Well, they get stuck up this rock with all the soldiers round them and they have to stay there all day getting baked in the sun and then they get off and they run again and hide and only have cold porridge to eat. And now they've been captured by another clan man called Cluny Macpherson and he makes them play cards and wins all Davy's money. It's good. It's like us. Running and hiding and surviving.'

I was tired and Peppa put her light out and fell asleep. I lay there and thought for a while. I was thinking about Ingrid's life but mostly about her mother. Her maw probably got murdered by a Russian and she didn't think about it much at all afterwards. Did she love her? It made me think about Maw and all the things I did to look after her. From even when I was really wee I was always making sure she was alright and she had her cans or her bottle and cleaning up and making sure nobody knew about the drinking or her being asleep. I used to tell people she was working night shifts and she had to sleep all day. I had to watch her too and make sure she didn't be sick laying on her back because you can choke to death on your vomit. And I had to watch Peppa because when Peppa was really wee she used to climb in and sleep with Maw and I worried Maw would roll on her and suffocate her which can happen but it is not as common as people think.

Maw didn't do anything when Robert hit her. Or when he hit us. She just cried really quiet and said 'Robert, no.' Once I got up when they were in a rammy and Robert had her by the hair and was dragging her round the front room and laughing. I jumped on his back to stop him and he punched me in the face and made my lips bleed. And Maw just kept going 'Robert. No' over and over again. But it was because she was drinking and drinking makes you accept the unacceptable. Now she was sober she'd see what was wrong with it all.

She got worse after Robert came. He liked her drinking and he got her cider and vodka and cans all the time. If she tried to not drink or just have Coke he said 'Don't be so fucking stupid Claire.' And once he forced her to drink from a bottle of vodka when she said she wasn't going to drink because it was Peppa's birthday and she wanted to be sober when we got home from school. She was drunk when we got back and she kept saying 'I'm sorry baby. Robert made me drink. He made me drink the vodka. He forced us!' and Robert was laughing and he went 'Aye I did.' And she laughed too.

That night I made Peppa proper burgers out of mince while Robert and Maw were out of it and I used seeded baps like real burgers and burger sauce made from tomato ketchup and mayonnaise, and she said 'Just like McDonald's.' Then I told her about the Nachthexen who I had just read about on Wikipedia and she loved it and she said what does it mean? I told her 'Nacht' meant night in German and 'Hexen' meant witches and she said 'Nachthexen – nice word.'

Chapter Twelve

Magna Bra

The next day we got up early and got the fire roaring and made porridge and tea and Ingrid said she was going to Magna Bra. She had a big purple hat on and had a long stick and had all coloured ribbons and scarves in her hair and loads of make-up. Peppa said she looked like a wizard and I thought she looked more like a witch than before. She said 'I go to speak to the Goddess.'

We went with her and I took the monocular and the airgun in case I saw some birds or rabbits. It was a long climb up through the woods and there was new snow on the moor. We went through a little stand of old Scots pines which had snow on them and the sun came out and it was bright and white and like Christmas in films. Once all of Scotland was covered in Scots pine forests but they were all cut down by people to burn and make houses out of. Scots pines grow big and some in forests twist over and bend like old men to get light. In spring they give pine resin that burns and Ingrid tapped them and collected it.

Going up over the moor towards the high ground Ingrid told us what she believed.

'I believe there is a Mother Goddess who controls all of nature and the world. In fact all of nature is the Mother Goddess and she nurtures and creates all life. You can talk to her and you can feel her warmth in the sun and in the earth in spring. You can feel her skin in soft grass and the fur of animals and the feathers of birds. You can taste her in the food you get from nature and the sweet water from a stream. You can smell her in the pine forest and the dying leaves and the honeysuckle and in oak leaves in the rain. You can hear her voice in birdsong and the wind in the trees, in the snow creaking under your boots and in owls' cries. And you can see her in the rolling hills and the moor and . . .'

And she stopped and turned to us and smiled and held her finger up 'In *your* face Peppa. And in *your* face Sal. And in *my* face. And in the faces of all women.'

Then she started off again striding away with her stick and she said 'I go to feel her in the stones and ask for her blessing and ask for her to lead me to forgiveness for all the things I did wrong in my life.'

Peppa said 'What's her name?'

Ingrid said 'She has no name. She is unnameable. And unknowable. But you can feel her.'

Peppa said 'We should give her a name.'

I was listening. And then I stopped Ingrid and said 'Will she forgive my maw?'

Ingrid said 'Of course. She is forgiveness because she has never condemned. We condemn ourselves Sal. She judges nobody.'

'But you said she would forgive like God. And my maw needs to be forgiven for not being a proper mother.'

Ingrid said 'Do you forgive her?'

I thought about it. And I said 'Not if she drinks again. I forgive her for having an illness.'

Ingrid looked at Peppa who was bounding on ahead and swinging her arms and singing. 'Does Peppa forgive her?'

I said 'She didn't do anything to Peppa and I was there to look after Peppa so she doesn't have to forgive her. And Peppa loves her. She wants us to go and get her and bring her to the forest.'

Ingrid sat down on a rock and looked at me. 'The Goddess will make your mother see that she needs to forgive herself and you need to forgive yourself too.'

I said 'Why? I haven't done anything wrong. I killed my maw's boyfriend who was called Robert but that wasn't wrong. He hit my maw and he hit me and Peppa. And since I was ten he made me suck his cock whenever he wanted to. And he said he was going to start making Peppa do it. So I stabbed him in the throat. Three times and we ran and hid. And I fixed it so they couldn't blame Maw.'

Ingrid put her arms around me and hugged me and held me close to her and I thought I was going to greet again. Then she said 'You did nothing wrong. And the Goddess will give you strength and love.'

Peppa was shouting down at us from up on a ridge and waving and then she sprinted down towards us grinning.

'Let's call her Cheryl!' she said.

And Ingrid thought for a minute and said okay.

It was still and bright at the stones and there was no breeze. The cold air was soft and hung over them and the snow sparkled like jewels. Ingrid stood right in the middle and held up her hands and whispered in German. I walked right round each stone and tried to feel something but all I felt was the sharp cold in my lungs as I breathed in. Then I felt a rumbly feeling in my belly and a tickly pain shooting down. It went all wet and warm in my pants. I pulled my trousers out and looked and saw blood. I stood there for quite a while feeling it getting warm and drippy in there. I didn't have any Always Ultra with me.

Peppa came running up and said 'You alright Sal?'

I said 'I've got my period . . .'

Peppa went 'Whooooaaa! Ingrid! Sal's got her period!' in a really loud voice and then danced off across the snow.

Ingrid ran over to me and said 'Sal. That is wonderful! It is wonderful! It is the Goddess! You are a woman!'

I said 'I need an Always Ultra. I'm in a right mess Ingrid . . .' The blood was starting to ooze down my legs. Ingrid pulled off her silk scarf that she used for the sphagnum moss and said 'Use this.'

And I stuffed it down my pants to soak it all up. Ingrid put her arms round me again. She said 'It is magic. You are magic Sal.'

Peppa came running past and said 'You can have a baby now Sal!' and then ran off round the stones.

We walked back down and I started feeling sore and horrible and my belly ached. Ingrid walked with her arm round me and Peppa carried the stick and the airgun.

We got back to the camp and Ingrid boiled a big pan of water and I washed by the fire and got an Always Ultra and put on clean pants and joggers and a vest and a jumper and a fleece. Ingrid put three big potatoes in the embers of the fire to cook. I burned my bloody pants in the fire and put my trousers in the burn pool to soak. We sat by the fire while the potatoes cooked and then we had them with butter and beans and bread. My belly was sore and I had an ibuprofen and codeine, and Ingrid wrapped a hot rock in a towel and I held it on my belly and it felt nice.

By the fire, Ingrid got a blanket and wrapped me up

and I stared into the flames and watched the wood glowing almost white in the middle of it, then yellow and orange and then dull red and then black and wee blue flames flicking out of the orange and running along the logs. I could feel the heat on my face and the warmth in my belly from the stone. My mind went all slow and was not racing thinking and I breathed in the cold air and the smoke from the sticks.

Ingrid washed all the pots in the stream and then stacked them by the fire to dry and Peppa got a blanket and wrapped it round her and sat on a log and read with her light. It was getting dark. It was getting dark earlier and earlier and I realised we were in November.

Ingrid got a log and sat next to me and put her arm around me and I leaned onto her shoulder and she cuddled me. I used to hate people touching me but I liked Ingrid cuddling me.

Then Ingrid said 'We shall go and get your mother?'

Peppa looked up from her book and said 'Can we Sal?'

Ingrid said 'Where is she?'

I said 'She is in an alcoholic rehab place. They put her in there after we ran to get her sober. It's near here. It's twenty-six miles away.'

Peppa said 'Is it? Can we go now?'

Ingrid said 'If she wants to leave she can. They are voluntary facilities. Does she know where you are?'

I said 'No. She thinks we might be dead.'

Ingrid said 'Well, if she is undergoing a detox and a rehabilitation it usually takes about four weeks. But after this she will need to have support and go to addiction meetings like Alcoholics Anonymous or Narcotics Anonymous where they have a programme of group therapy which can be a very effective treatment.'

I said 'If she is sober she could come and live here with us. We could look after her.'

Peppa got up and started dancing about excited. 'We can make her a bender and teach her to skin rabbits!'

I said 'Can you see Maw skinning rabbits Peppa?'

Peppa said 'How can we get her without you being caught Sal? If they see me or you we'll get nicked and split up and taken off Maw . . .'

Ingrid said 'We can get a car. We can drive to the place. We can watch it. We can wait till we see her. Does she smoke cigarettes?'

I said 'Aye.'

Ingrid went on. 'So. We watch. We wait until she comes outside to smoke. They all go outside to smoke in those places. And when she comes outside I will speak to her and ask her if she wishes to come with us. I will do it secretly. Nobody will know. Then she can slip out and meet us. And then we can come back here.'

I said 'Where do we get a car?'

Ingrid said 'I will steal one. From the garage on the main road. As long as it is old I can start it.'

Peppa was going 'Yesss . . . Oh please Sal. Let's do that.'

I said 'I've got a map where it is.'

Ingrid said 'Perfect.'

I said 'How do you steal a car?'

Ingrid said 'You need a piece of copper wire and a screwdriver. And a hammer to break the window. My boyfriend taught me to do it in the eighties.'

Peppa said 'Did you have a boyfriend? Was he good-looking?'

I said 'Can you teach me to do it?'

Ingrid laughed and clapped her hands. 'Can I tell you the last bit of my story?'

We said yes. And Peppa went and got Ingrid a blanket.

They interviewed her for weeks and weeks after she defected. And they gave her a flat in London to live in and she had to tell them everything she knew about the GDR and the SED. She told them all about her research work and the people she knew in Berlin and the Stasi. One of the men interviewing her said 'You are in danger. The Stasi sometimes execute defectors abroad to make an example. It has never happened in the UK but there is always a first time.'

Ingrid lived in the flat in London on her own and went to a medical school for a year to learn how to be a doctor in the NHS in Britain. For a while British spies followed her and listened to her phone when she made calls but soon they stopped. They thought she might be a spy pretending to be a defector. But she wasn't.

She was on her own·all the time and soon she got depressed and started thinking a lot about when she was wee and the things that happened in her flat. And about leaving Germany and not building socialism like she wanted to when she was young. She thought about her mum and she tried to remember Latvian but she couldn't. She thought about how scared she was when there was bombing and the Russians came. And she got more and more depressed and then she had a breakdown when she went mad and cried all the time and wanted to kill herself. She got put in a hospital for mad people and treated with drugs and she had therapy and talked a lot about her life and especially about her mum and how she felt about the things she had seen and done.

She was in the hospital for two years. It was in a nice big house in the countryside and after two years she was better and they let her leave and she got a job as a doctor in a hospital in a small town. She looked after people who had things like diabetes and cancer and heart attacks.

She still liked hippies and she liked pop music and she started going to festivals where bands played and everyone took drugs and she met a load of hippies and she bought a VW van and went camping at festivals in the summer. They went to Stonehenge which is big old standing stones in the middle of a heath in England where the sun rises over a special stone on Midsummer Day and all the hippies and druids go there and get wasted and sing and dance. She felt best and not at all depressed when she was there with all the hippies and soon she was going to meet them every weekend and she met a man called Matt who was younger than her and had dreadlocks. She became his girlfriend although she said she was old enough to be his mother.

There was a thing then called the Peace Convoy and it was loads of hippies who lived in old vans and buses and they drove round England and camped wherever they liked and went to festivals. There were hundreds of them all living in big camps making music and making baskets and things out of wood and selling them and getting broo money off the government and just staying in the country and not having houses.

And eventually Ingrid joined them. She gave up her job as a doctor and she took her van and went and lived with the hippies. Her and Matt drove round with them in big long lines of vans and buses and when they stopped she looked after people who were ill and helped the hippie girls have their babies. The hippies called her the Defector Doctor and they painted it on her van. She made lots of them better mostly from things like infections and skin rashes but sometimes from taking drugs too much.

They lived on land that was owned by lords and rich farmers, and the police used to come and harass them all the time. Sometimes they blocked off roads to stop them getting places and they were always arresting them for drugs or having bald tyres on their vans.

Ingrid learned a lot of things living with the hippies. She learned to make fires without matches and how to weave baskets from willow, she learned about tapping pine for resin and how to dig clay and make pots you baked in a fire to make them waterproof. She bought all her clothes from charity shops and let her hair go long and wild and she wore feathers and flowers and ribbons in it.

She learned all about mending a car from Matt who was a mechanic and he showed her how to hot-wire a car so you could start it without having the keys. She learned to change tyres and fix the brakes and once her and Matt even took the whole engine out of her VW van and fixed the gearbox.

She loved Matt. He was big and he didn't wash much and Ingrid used to make him jump in rivers if they were near one and she always boiled water and washed herself and her clothes because she didn't like being smelly.

Then after she had been with the hippies for about two years and they had been all over England to different festivals and living at different campsites they tried to get to Stonehenge for a festival on the summer solstice which was June 21st and is the longest day. Lots of vans and buses tried to drive to Stonehenge for the solstice but the police blocked all the roads and they held them all up and stopped them leaving and then they made lots of them drive into a field. It was a warm summer afternoon and the hippies got into a big crowd and tried to walk over to Stonehenge to try to have their festival.

And then hundreds of polis with riots shields and batons attacked them. There were about seven hundred hippies and twice as many police who had come from all over Britain to beat them up. They charged into them with police horses and batons and smashed people's heads and hit women and children and even pregnant women. Ingrid got punched in the face by a polis when she was trying to help a girl back into her bus. The polis surrounded all the hippie buses and smashed the windows and slashed the tyres and smashed them all up. Ingrid and Matt got arrested and Matt had his arm broken by two polis who kicked the shit out of him while he was lying on the ground. Ingrid fought two polis trying to take him away and she got kicked over and then handcuffed.

Hundreds of the hippies got arrested and they were all taken to stations in towns nearby and held and charged with obstructing the polis and assault on the polis. It was the most people who had ever been arrested in one go in the history of England. Ingrid said the papers called it 'The Battle of the Beanfield' but Ingrid said it was more like a massacre.

Then they let them all go, and Ingrid and Matt walked back to the field and found their van which had been smashed up and had all the windscreen broken. They eventually got their van going and they drove off and left the rest of the hippies. Matt had to go to hospital and have his arm put in plaster. Then they camped outside a small town for a few days and Matt got some bits and fixed the van up and they decided to go north.

The government put fences up around Stonehenge and

built a visitors' centre and charged people money to go and look at the stones and no hippies were allowed to go there ever again.

After that Ingrid got depressed again. She thought Britain was safe and the polis were nice here and didn't attack people for no reason and didn't put them in prison for nothing or force them to go where they didn't want to. She thought that only happened in the GDR or in Germany when there were Nazis, but it was happening in Britain which was a democracy and which she thought was free and people were allowed to do what they liked.

She got more and more depressed as they went north. They stayed in the Lake District for a few weeks in a layby and Matt got them some money by working in a garage fixing cars. Then some men from the council made them move and said they'd get arrested if they stayed in the layby.

Ingrid said they headed for Scotland because there is a different law in Scotland and you can camp wherever you like and you can't be moved on or arrested as long as you don't make a mess or burn down trees.

She was still depressed and they struggled to get money for food and petrol and it was coming on winter, but the country was beautiful. Much more beautiful than England and it had proper mountains and bigger lochs and moors. Ingrid said she had never been anywhere as beautiful and she liked Scottish people although she didn't understand the way they spoke at first. They got all the way into the Highlands and found places to camp and stay in their van and they spent the first winter in a forest near Fort William and they could see Ben Nevis from their van window. It snowed and it was cold but they had a wood burner in their van and they got broo money after a while.

Matt got a job working in the forest cutting logs and

trees with a chainsaw and driving a big tree-cutting machine. Then they rented a wee cottage for a few months and they had more room and a proper bed and Ingrid made clothes and did basket weaving.

In the spring they fixed the van up and went off again and drove all over Scotland and then got ferries to the Orkney Islands and went and saw all the standing stones and the 4,000-year-old houses and the burial chambers where old chiefs of tribes got buried with all their families.

They stayed in Orkney for a winter in their van and Matt worked for a farmer and Ingrid made baskets and sometimes sold them in the town. But it rained all the time for the whole winter. Ingrid sometimes got depressed because the days were so short and Matt sometimes went into the town and went to the pub with lads he worked with on the farm. Ingrid didn't go because she was older than all of them and she thought Matt should be with lads his own age.

In the spring they came back onto the mainland and went south and west and back through the Highlands and then down through Argyll and they went to Mull for a few months where the sea was clear and green and the sun shone all day. They lived on a beach there and swam and collected mussels and clams and crabs to eat. matt went fishing and caught mackerel and at night they had big driftwood fires on the beach. Once a fisherman gave them a huge bag of big prawns he couldn't sell and they cooked them on hot stones on the beach watching the sun go down over the sea. Ingrid said it was the best food she had ever eaten in her life.

In the autumn they went south again and drove down through Ayrshire and into Galloway and went to the Isle of Whithorn which is the furthest south you can get in Scotland and you can see England, Ireland and the Isle of Man.

Then they went back up into Galloway and drove into the Galloway forest. There were forestry roads you could use to get right into the forest and up and away from everyone and everything and they spent the first winter not far from where Ingrid's camp is now.

Ingrid worried about Matt because he was so young and she was getting near fifty and she knew he loved children and he wanted to have them. But he loved her and he was kind and funny and he looked after her and he was so strong he could lift their VW up at one end. She knew that one day he'd go and leave her and probably find another woman who was younger than her. And in a way she didn't mind because it seemed like it was natural.

They walked a lot round the forest and the moors and went to Magna Bra and they collected wood and snared rabbits and fished in the lochs. They sometimes went into the town and after a few months they started getting broo money. Ingrid read a lot of books she got from the library and second-hand book shops about medicine and science and she read about God and religion and she read stories as well. She liked a book called *Wuthering Heights* by Emily Brontë and she liked books by Charles Dickens about orphans and people in the workhouse.

In the spring when the leaves were all new and bright green Matt said he wanted to leave and go back to England. Ingrid wanted to stay in Scotland because they never got bothered by polis or the council in Scotland and she loved the forest and the hills they lived in. She told Matt it was okay for him to go and he cried and then he went.

Ingrid stayed in the van on her own for a few weeks and then she went to the town and rented a little house by the river and decided she'd stay there for a few years. She got her rent paid by the council and she got broo money and she read a lot. After about two years there she decided she could become a doctor again and she wrote letters to a council that give doctors licences and she had to go to Glasgow for a year and do another course and work in a hospital and then she got her licence to be a doctor again.

Then she heard that the old doctor in the town in Galloway had died and they needed a new one and she applied and got the job of being the doctor in a little surgery in the main street and she moved back, got a wee house to live in and became the doctor. She was fifty-three.

She stayed being the doctor there for the next fourteen years. She stopped wearing hippie clothes and started looking normal and had her hair cut and wore proper coats and shoes, not boots. She made friends with people in the town and they all liked her. Most of the old people thought that because she had a funny accent she was English but they were still nice to her and she was a good doctor and she read about medicine all the time and went on courses to learn about new treatments. She didn't get depressed as much and she almost never thought about when she was wee or the GDR or Max or defecting or the Battle of the Beanfield or Matt. By then the GDR had stopped being called the GDR and it was just all Germany and the Berlin Wall had been taken down and people didn't have to defect. Ingrid decided she didn't want to go back and see Berlin because she was happy being the doctor in the town and living in her wee house. She had a garden and grew vegetables and she made friends with an old man called Donald who lived near her and liked growing vegetables. His wife had died of cancer and he was lonely and he and Ingrid became a bit like boyfriend and girlfriend except they were old. Donald took her fishing with flies on the River Cree and she caught Salmon and he showed her how to tie fishing flies. She looked after him because he had a bad heart and couldn't run or eat butter. They talked a lot and told each other about their lives and he had been in the army in Germany in the 1960s when they built the Berlin Wall and he could speak a bit of German and she taught him more. Donald had an old dog called Kipper and they walked him all over the place and sometimes went up into the forest and let Kipper chase rabbits.

They listened to old hippie music from the 1960s and sometimes they danced in her wee house and Donald pretended he was playing guitar solos.

Donald asked her to marry him but she said she was too old to get married and she liked being single anyway and Donald said people in the town gossiped about them and she said 'I don't care.' She loved Donald in a different way to the way she loved Matt and Max, she loved him more like he was a nice dog you could cuddle.

Ingrid taught herself to make bread and she bought a kiln and made pots in her shed on a potting wheel and painted them and then fired them in the kiln so they shone. She made Donald a model of Kipper with the same white and black fur and big floppy ears. Donald grew vegetables for them and on a Sunday they had a Sunday dinner of roast beef and all Donald's vegetables and they used to set a place at the table for Kipper and let him have his dinner with them.

Ingrid saw lots of people die being a doctor and she had to sign death certificates. It made her think about her mother whenever anyone died, especially if it was a woman. She didn't even know if her mother did die or if she just ran off or got taken to Russia.

When someone dies, the second when they stop being alive, all the energy in them goes up out of them. It is like a cloud you cannot see rising up above them. I saw it go out of Robert when he was bleeding and going 'ock' on my bed. Something that was there but not there went out of him and went up and he was dead. Then he was just meat bleeding.

Ingrid said she saw this lots and lots of times and she said it was the soul going back to its mother. The soul is the thing that makes you alive and a person and Ingrid said that everything that is alive has a soul and even things that are not alive like rocks and earth have a soul. And souls are born from the Mother Goddess and they vibrate at different frequencies and have different amounts of light in them depending on how much they vibrate. What you see leaving a dead person is their vibration. You see and feel the vibration of them and you only know it is there when it is gone.

Some souls vibrate so much they glow when they leave and some souls vibrate slow and dark and are like slugs leaving. Robert's was like that. It oozed out of him.

Some people have souls that vibrate so much they give off light when they are alive. Peppa is like that. Sometimes at night in the shelter when it is pitch dark I can feel her glow.

If Robert's soul went up to the Mother Goddess I hope she told it to fuck off.

Ingrid was happy for quite a few years in the town with Donald and Kipper and then Kipper got ill and died and Donald was really depressed. And then one day Donald was pouring a cup of tea in Ingrid's kitchen and he went all floppy and held onto his chest and fell off the kitchen chair and died. Ingrid watched his soul go up while she was banging his chest to get his heart going again.

After that she got depressed again for a long time and thought a lot about when she was wee and about all the people she'd known. She got too old to be the doctor in the town and she got a pension and retired. She was lonely without Donald and Kipper and she started going into the forest a lot and sitting in the trees and thinking about the Goddess. She thought about when she'd been a hippie and about when she'd been wee in the cellar with Klausi and Hansi. She thought about the days looking for her mother in all the bombed streets in Berlin. She thought about Max leaving her and about the Stasi arresting him and executing him. She thought about immunology and all the things she knew how to do.

Then she decided she was going to go and live in the forest. She had quite a lot of money in the bank and she could've bought a house but she didn't want to. She wanted to live in the forest in a bender and trap food and walk and have fires at night under the stars. So she did. She sold all the things she owned and gave her car to her next-door neighbour. She gave most of her clothes to the charity shop and bought boots and a big waxed coat and some hats and a knife. Then she walked up into the forest and made a camp and lived there.

And then she met us.

Chapter Thirteen

Skis

Me and Peppa went up to the lochs with the fishing rod and some spinners and hooks. Ingrid was feeling tired and said her back ached because she had been stamping on sticks to break them to the right length to go on the drying rack.

It was cold and the snow was thicker the higher we got and we skirted round the edge of the forest at the top and followed it to a ridge and from there you could see a chain of lochs going off along a valley that was all white and shiny.

I sat on the ridge and watched it all through the monocular which magnifies things by a factor of four for every ten metres. There was an eagle over the lochs hanging high up like it was still in the air. It had white tips on its wings and the wings had feathers that looked like long fingers coming out of a hand. In the monocular you could see the feathers vibrating in the air.

Peppa ran on down the long slope to the first loch and kept jumping and sliding along on her bum on the snow. She looked like an emperor penguin in her black Helly Hansen whooshing along getting smaller and smaller as she went down. I watched her through the monocular and I could see she was grinning and shouting and laughing every time she started sliding. It made me glad I had killed Robert and it made me want to get Maw so she could see Peppa laughing in the snow.

I went down after her and the loch was frozen over with grey furry ice that had big white bubbles in it. Peppa was walking out on it and I shouted her to be careful. The ice cracked and creaked when you stepped on it. You could walk on it alright if you stayed by the edge and I told Peppa not to go out any further than me. We slid along it. Sometimes white jagged cracks suddenly shot out from under our feet and there was a sound like metal hitting on metal. It was no good for fishing but we slid along it all the way to the end and then Peppa got pebbles and skidded them out along onto it so they spun and shot right into the middle. It was shallow under the ice and you could see the grey and brown pebbles on the bottom, just a few inches below the surface.

She knelt down on the ice and looked down to the bottom where you see pebbles and the water all clear through the ice. Then she sat and slid along on her bum. She spun herself round and round like the stones. Then she pointed across behind me and said 'There's a man.'

I spun round and a man was coming towards us from the other side of the loch on skis. He was shuffling along and pushing through the snow on a flat bit coming straight up to us. I didn't know what to do and I started feeling panicky. Peppa sat on the ice watching him squinting up into the sun.

He got nearer and nearer and we saw he was young and had short blond hair and ski goggles. He was wearing a blue zipper and had white ski gloves and boots. He was puffing and blowing and sending big curls of white breath in front of him. He was grinning with the effort of pushing himself along.

I didn't know if we should run or not, but he was almost level with us and he had seen us and what was the point. Then he stopped and pulled the goggles up and let out a big long groan and shook his head so his hair flopped around.

He was smiling and he shouted over 'Whoa. Hard work! How are ya?'

I didn't say anything. I just stared. Peppa just sat on the ice.

He nodded at the loch and he was starting to unclip his skis. 'Frozen pretty solid eh?' He glanced down at the rock where I'd left the fishing rod and said 'Not much good for fishing is it?'

He was English and he was posh. He'd unclipped his skis now and he walked over the snow to the ice and just started talking like we knew him.

'Come all the way over from Glentrool. Pretty hard going this last bit. Going back over that way – past the stones, bit more slopey down there.'

Peppa stood up and was looking at him. He was good-looking. His hair was that kind of reddy blond and it was all fluffy and wispy round his face. He had big eyes and his lips were thick and pink. He had pink cheeks and his eyelashes were long and dark. He walked onto the ice and stamped and a big crack opened and shot out away from him with a hissing sound and he jumped back and went 'Whoa! Cool!'

He stamped again and the big chunk of ice flipped up and clattered away from the hole he made and water bubbled out. He kicked at the ice lump and it spun and skidded across to where Peppa was and he went 'Yeah! Ice hockey!'

Peppa kicked it back and he slid away from her and stuck his leg out to stop it passing him and then kicked it back. Peppa was smiling and slid over and kicked it back. The lump flashed along the ice between them twirling silver in the sunshine.

I stepped back towards the shore and watched and they started kicking the ice lump and Peppa was laughing and shouting 'Nah!' when she missed it and he was smiling and shouting and gliding about. They were about twenty metres from each other and he pulled his goggles from round his neck and put them on the ice and then took off one of his gloves and put that down about two metres away and he shouted and pointed 'Hey! Goal!' and Peppa started sliding towards him pushing the ice in front of her like a football player. Then kicked it hard and it shot towards him in the goal and he stretched and then flipped up and crashed down onto his arse and he went 'Oooh.' The ice cracked where he hit it and water blew out along the crack and he scrabbled and slipped trying to get back up. Peppa was still flying towards him and she hit the water and flipped over too. He was laughing and he had his hands down on the ice and his feet were sliding and slipping from under him as he tried to get up. Peppa was slipping and tripping and laughing and she bumped down onto the watery ice and went 'Aaah, ma bum's wet!'

He was sitting too now with his legs straight out in front of him and he said 'Me too. I'm Adam.' The sun was shining full on him and he smiled over at me. Peppa got up and skidded over to him. She said 'I'm Peppa. She's ma sister Sal' before I could stop her. Then she said 'Are you English?'

He held his hand out and she grabbed it and helped pull him up and he said 'Yeah. Are you Scottish?'

Peppa slid away from him back towards me on the shore and went 'Aye. We're on holiday.'

He came over slipping to the shore. He said 'Me too.

I'm staying with some people from uni other side of Glentrool. It's cool here isn't it?'

Peppa said 'Aye. Are you posh?'

He frowned for a second then smiled again and said 'Well no, I wouldn't say posh. I'm a student. I like cross-country skiing. And ice hockey on frozen lochs with funny little girls.'

Peppa was stood by me now and she almost half hid behind me and peeked round at him grinning. He looked at me and he was still smiling and putting his goggles back round his neck. He nodded at her and said to me 'She's a little ball of fire isn't she?'

I couldn't say anything. I didn't even know what he meant and I just kept staring at him. He had gold freckles on his forehead and wee red blond hairs coming out of his chin where he hadn't shaved. He was tall and his shoulders were wide and he had big hands with long thin fingers. Peppa skipped out in front of me saying 'Have you got a girlfriend?'

He laughed, shaking the water out his ski glove and looked me in the eye and shook his head like he was saying 'Kids eh?' Peppa was right up by him now and she carried on, 'Have ye? Is she pretty?'

He grabbed her and started tickling her and she shrieked and he span her round and held her upside down. I just stood there not moving. Not even when he grabbed her. She was screaming and laughing and he put her down and she jumped up at him and he caught her again and she tapped on his chest with a pointy finger and went 'Well, laddie have ye, or no?'

He said 'Yes.'

She said 'Is she pretty?'

He said 'Not as pretty as you.'

She said 'What's her name?'

He said 'Hermione.'

Peppa laughed and jumped down from his arms and said 'What, like Harry Potter?' and he said 'Yes' and Peppa said 'Is she a witch?' and he said 'Yes.' Peppa said 'You're lying!'

He walked back over to his skis and started clipping them on. Peppa ran over to him again. She said 'Have you read *Kidnapped* by Robert Louis Stevenson?' He stopped and thought for a second and then said 'Yes I have. Davy and Alan.'

Peppa said 'Aye, that's me and Sal.'

He said 'Who's Davy?' and Peppa said 'Me' and he looked over at me smiling and said 'I'll have to be careful of Sal then – is she good with a sword?'

Peppa said 'No but she can use a knife, and shoot and snare rabbits and catch pike and build shelters and make fire. We're outlaws. You could be Sal's boyfriend. She's a woman. She's had a period.'

And then I did speak. I shouted 'PEPPA!' I was hot and my heart was banging and Peppa skipped off laughing. Adam was still smiling and shaking his head. He looked at me again and he looked kind and his eyes were soft and he said 'I've got a little sister just like her. They drive you mad don't they?'

I was still all hot and I just went 'Aye.'

Then Peppa shouted 'Snowball!' and a snowball hit Adam on the arm and he laughed and pulled his goggles on and started pushing off and he shouted 'Bye Peppa!' and she threw another snowball at him and shouted 'Bye Adam!' He stopped and pulled his goggles up and looked back at me and said 'Bye Sal.' And I said bye and he skied off up along the side of the loch where we'd come and then pushed up the slope towards the ridge and the moor.

Peppa came and stood by me and said 'I fancy him Sal. Do you?'

I said 'Come on.' And we started off back, walking in the tracks his skis had made. We watched him getting smaller and smaller as he pushed up the slope and finally disappeared over the ridge at the top. As we walked back up slowly Peppa said 'Will he tell on us?'

I said 'You shouldnae've told him our names Peppa. Or said we were outlaws.'

She said 'He won't tell. He's nice. And he's good-looking int he?'

'Just coz he's good-looking doesn't mean he's nice Peppa.'

Peppa said 'Aye it does. I like posh people. He had big muscles on his arms. Did you fancy him Sal?'

I said 'No.'

She said 'Aye you did. You went all red.'

I said 'Shut up Peppa.'

I don't like telling her to shut up but sometimes she pushes it. It's because Peppa thinks everything is funny and she can't be serious about anything and sometimes she doesn't realise you shouldn't push people just because you think things are funny. But she is only ten. Most things are serious and you have to make plans and Peppa doesn't understand that yet. She was too wee to remember a lot of things in the flat or I stopped her seeing them or being there when Maw was really bad or when Robert was there and hitting her and coming in my room at night. But sometimes you just have to take action and sort things out and get everything in order. Just like with a camp when you are surviving. If a camp is ordered and tidy and well planned you will survive and your morale will be better.

At the top of the ridge we could see Adam's ski tracks going off away from us and our woods over the moor where it dipped down in a low valley and then rose again towards Magna Bra. It was coming dark and the sun was going pink in the west over the tops of the big Scots pines. I decided there was no point in worrying about him telling. And he didn't know where we were anyway and Ingrid's was impossible to find if you didn't know where to look.

Back at the camp Ingrid had the fire going and had made bread and soup, but she was hobbling with her back and after we'd had tea she sat in front of me on a long log and I rubbed her back at the bottom where it hurt her. She took some ibuprofen and codeine and then I held a hot stone in a towel on her back for her. Then she got me to get snow and rub it all over her back to freeze it. Her skin was smooth on her back and she smelled of pine. Then I put the hot stone on again. She said it was a way of freeing trapped nerves and getting blood circulating. She said 'It is slower with me because I am old now.' Then I rubbed her back more and massaged it and she said 'Gut. You have healing hands Sal.'

We sat by the fire and it started to get really cold so we wrapped up in blankets and Peppa wore her rabbit hat. We talked about getting Maw again and Ingrid said we should do it soon before her back got worse. I thought we should try and get her soon too. She would be coming up four weeks sober and they might send her away from the rehab soon. Peppa said we should make her a bender so we decided we'd do that the next day and then the day after that we'd go and get her.

Chapter Fourteen

Car

We were cold that night and in the end I got a rock from the fire and wrapped it in a towel and we had it in bed in between us and it worked. In the morning I got up and got the fire going and made the porridge and tea and then I went and cut poles for Maw's bender.

It was hard work and we let Ingrid stay in bed and rest her back while we got the poles and piled up rocks to make a plinth for the bed. I had to cut a lot of spruce branches for the covering because it had to be thick, we had no tarp to cover it. I spent all day dragging the spruce back and Peppa and me thatched it thick. If it snowed again it would be good to insulate it more. Maw's bender was near the fire on the river side and looked back at ours and Ingrid's. It looked like a real Indian camp with three of them round the fire in the middle. Peppa swept all the snow and leaves out off the floor and we put spruce down thick and treaded it flat and we made her a table out of flat rocks and Ingrid gave us more blankets and a quilt for the bed. Peppa made a star out of feathers and ribbons and we hung it over the doorway and it looked really nice. We hung a big piece of green cloth Ingrid gave us over the doorway and we put some of Ingrid's birch bark candles in there and Ingrid gave us a basket she could have on her table to put all her bits in. We put some of Ingrid's scarves over the bed covers to make it look nice too.

Ingrid's back hurt all day and she said she'd be alright if she rested so she did. We had rice and beans and bread to eat and lots of tea with sugar. I was starting to get excited about Maw coming to the camp and living with us.

The next day we all got up and Ingrid said her back was fine but she still walked slower. She got a screwdriver, a bit of copper wire and a little hammer out of one her boxes and then put them in the pocket of her big coat. She didn't wear a hat, she wore some of her scarves tied up in her hair.

I got the backpack and brought the maps and the compass and my knife and my monocular.

We had porridge and tea and then used the two head torches and set off down towards the road before it started getting light. It was slippy going down through the wood and we saw the badger running back towards his sett in the wee woody valley over the river in the half light.

We came out just up from the garage and the Little Chef but stayed in the woods and went along the road and then into the car park at the back and Peppa and me stood in the trees and Ingrid said 'I have to find an old car. I cannot start a new car. I can only start old cars. Like a VW or a Volvo.' So she walked out into the car park. There were already cars in it and the lights were on in the Little Chef and the garage but you couldn't see the car park from the entrance. We watched as Ingrid walked around the car park looking at all the cars. Sometimes she bent down and looked hard at the bumper or the back of one. Then she disappeared into a row over by the exit and then we saw her stand up and walk towards us smiling with both her thumbs up.

We ran across towards her and as we did I heard a little bang and then a rattling sound. We got to the car and saw she had busted the window with her little hammer and there were squares of glass all over the tarmac by the door. She pulled the lock thing on the door and opened it quickly and then reached back and pulled locks on the back door and said 'Get in.'

She was crouching down under the steering wheel and there were ripping and banging sounds for a few seconds and then she was muttering in German. Me and Peppa sat in the back seat which was wide and covered in red leather. The car was nice and old, it had silver paint and the seats were all smooth and soft. There were two fleecy checked blankets on the back seat and Peppa snuggled up in hers and I sat up looking back out of the window in case anyone came. Then Ingrid went 'Aha!' and then we heard the car start and rumble and she jumped into the driver seat and slammed her door. She turned and said 'Gut! We have a car!' and Peppa went 'Yeaaahhh! Let's go and get Maw!'

Ingrid was fiddling and pulling at the knobs and the car lights came on and then she went 'Handbremse . . . aha . . . yah' and we went off backwards and then she clunked about again and we started going forwards and I watched as we pulled out past the Little Chef and onto the main road.

The car was big and it smelled lovely and it had nice polished wood on all the doors and wee tables in the seats. I climbed over the box thing in the middle and got in the front with Ingrid. It had a long silver bonnet and a silver angel with wings like she was flying at the end.

I said 'Posh car Ingrid.'

She said 'It is a Rolls-Royce. About nineteen eighty. Very

good. Automatic. Power steering. But no seat belts so I must be very careful. I will stay at exactly the speed limit.'

Peppa was sliding about on the back seat and rolling around in the blanket and she shouted 'It's lovely. Maw will love it.'

As we drove along I got the map out and started checking the signs we saw and worked out we were about twenty-two miles from where we turned off. Ingrid looked happy driving along with the wind blowing her hair through the smashed window.

There were almost no other cars on the road. We saw a few lorries coming the other way. The snow got less and less as we went along but the road sparkled with frost. We had to go out round a gritting lorry and then Ingrid drove along in front of it.

It would take us about twenty-five minutes to get to the turn-off we wanted for the Abbey which was near a village called Killaggan. I watched for the signs and felt the lovely gliding feeling of going along in the car. A car came up behind us and Ingrid watched it in her mirror and it went out and round us and carried on and she said 'Gut. Not police.'

Two more cars passed us and they weren't polis either and soon we had got near our turn-off and I watched and saw the sign for Killaggan and Ingrid turned and we went up a long straight road with trees either side. We had to watch for another road that went off from it before the village on the right. It was all woods around us and we found the next turn and it was like a wee lane and we went slow along it and over a humpy bridge. The lane turned a lot and Ingrid went slow in the big car. It was light now and there was white frost on everything.

We followed the wee road for about two miles and then

there was another wee road we turned up on the right and it went along by fields with woods round them and a dry-stane dyke. A bit further along and we saw a wooden sign that said 'THE ABBEY – TREATMENT CENTRE'.

There were stone gateposts and a drive going into the woods. We stopped and Ingrid said 'We need to hide the car and walk.'

We drove up a wee bit and found a flat grassy bit where we pulled in by some bushes and Ingrid put the car right in so the bushes hung over it. She said 'Get some branches. We hide it.' We got out and it was cold and quiet and still. Crows were squawking and that was it. Ingrid said 'Get branches.'

Peppa and me went into the woods and we started pulling branches out. I got a big dead branch of a beech tree that had brown leaves on it. We piled the branches up along the side of the car by the lane. Peppa pulled some ferns up and spread them over the back of it so you couldn't see the silver of the bumpers. We worked quick running in and pulling out twiggy branches and snapping off bits of beech with brown leaves still on them.

Ingrid walked out back into the lane and looked and said 'It is good. But our tracks are on the frost.' There were two tyre marks coming along the lane in the frost where we had drove up. She rubbed at them with her feet then said 'The sun will melt it away soon.'

I told Peppa to bring the blankets from the car and I brought the backpack and we walked back towards the gate and then went into the woods and walked down through the trees till we came to the wall. It was about 1.5 metres high running through the woods. Peppa just jumped up on it and down the other side, but I had to help Ingrid over it and then we dropped down into the woods that ran along the driveway. We crept along, and through the trees you could see a big grassy lawn with a wishing well in the middle and then the house. It was old with a pointy roof and wee battlements like a castle. The roof was green with moss on the slates. There was a stone entrance bit and there were lights on in some of the windows. At the front there were four cars parked on the gravel.

We went on through the woods that went all around the lawns of the house and at the back was a new bit sticking out with big sliding doors and a patio with tables and chairs like outside a pub.

Ingrid whispered 'There. That is where they will smoke.'

We got down and sat on one of the blankets behind the trees and some big bushes with thick green leaves and we could see the patio and the back doors. Peppa wrapped a blanket round her and we sat and watched and waited.

The sun came up over the house and made a big triangle on the lawn on the other side from us. We stayed quiet and watched. After about an hour some lights came on in the windows and went off and then a big light came on in the room behind the sliding doors. Someone slid them open and two men came out. A wee guy in a leather jacket and a bigger man wearing a tartan coat and holding a tea cup. They both sat on the benches and lit fags and we watched. Then a big fat woman came out and was talking to them and then she went in. Then the men finished their fags and went in and slid the doors shut.

It was quiet again. We waited. It seemed like another hour and then two women came out and stood on the patio looking out into the trees over the lawn and talking and one put her arm around the other one. They were too far to hear what they were saying. One woman had long dark hair and the other had really short blonde hair and was wearing a long grey coat. They stood there for a while and talked and then the woman in the grey coat walked out across the grass towards the trees. She turned and was talking to the other woman walking backwards over the lawn and you could see her breath going up in wee clouds. The other woman got some tobacco out and made a roll-up. She held it out to the other woman who walked back to her and took it. All the time she was talking and moving her arms up and down and holding her hands up like she was showing how big a fish was. She got the roll-up and lit it with a lighter and walked back out onto the lawn blowing smoke up and looking up at the trees. The other woman stayed on the patio and was talking and saying stuff to her and shaking her head. Then a big tall thin man with a beard came out and stood leaning on the wall by the sliding door and started saying things to them and then he pointed back in the house and then he went in.

The woman on the lawn was standing looking out at the trees and the other woman was shouting things over to her. You could just hear her voice but not the words. Then she turned and walked back in the house quick like she was angry. The woman on the lawn stayed looking at the trees and then she turned slowly looking all along the woods towards where we were. And Peppa whispered 'That's Maw!'

And I looked through the monocular and it was. Her hair was short and like a crop and yellow blond. But it was her. You could see the bulge of her big tits under the coat which was long and almost touched the ground. She stared over at the woods and it was like she was looking at us. Peppa went to get up and I grabbed her. 'I'll go and get her . . .' she whispered.

I said 'No, wait.'

Ingrid said 'I can go . . .'

But then she turned and threw the butt of her roll-up down and walked back towards the house and went in the doors.

I said 'It was her. She's changed her hair.'

Peppa said 'She's got a new coat. It's like a man's coat.'

It wasn't the sort of coat Maw would wear. She wore wee skinny leather jackets and jean jackets and she always wore heels and skirts. And her hair. She had long really nice brown hair and now it was all cropped and yellow.

Peppa whispered 'Her hair's like Niall out of One Direction Sal. Is she trying to look like a lad?'

Ingrid shifted up onto her knees and said 'My back is hurting me. I am sorry, I have to stand.'

She got up slowly and backed away from the edge of the trees into the wood and walked up and down stretching forward and holding her back at the bottom.

I watched the doors but nobody came out for ages. Peppa wrapped herself in a blanket and sat cross-legged and Ingrid lay flat out on the wood floor with her arms stretched up above her head. The sun was right up over the garden now and steam was rising off the frosty grass. It was really quiet again, just sometimes a crow, or a bird tweeting. Ingrid got onto all fours and started arching her back up and down and breathing on short puffs. Peppa leant against me with the blanket round her and I thought she might go to sleep and I just sat and watched the sliding doors through the monocular.

I could tell by the sun and the way the shadows of the trees were starting to get longer on the lawn that we had been waiting for about four hours, and then the sliding door opened and the woman that Maw had been with came out with the tall thin man and another guy with short white hair wearing a fleece. They all smoked and sat on the benches and I could hear little sounds of laughing from them. The thin guy stood up and was waving his arms around and looked like he was telling them a story and they were both laughing. Then we heard a car coming up the drive and stopping round at the front of the house and I got tense in case it was polis. Peppa heard it too and said 'I'll go and look' and she crept back along the way we'd come so she could see the front of the house. Ingrid was sitting with her eyes closed and her knees up under her chin. We heard Peppa coming back through the bushes and she sat down next to me and said 'It was a white van with a man bringing boxes in the front.'

The three of them on the benches were all standing now and looked like they were going back in. Then Maw came out again and she stood on the patio and they talked to her and she was shaking her head and kept putting her hands up to her mouth. We watched her. I wanted the others to go in and leave her out there but she didn't even have a fag and then went back in with them.

Peppa said 'This is stupid Sal. Let's just run in and find her.'

I said 'No Peppa. There's other people in there. They'll know it's us and they'll call the polis and we'll all get nicked.'

Ingrid crawled over to us and put her arms round us and said 'She will come out again. Don't worry. Relax. Let it happen. If she does not I will go in. Nobody knows me. I will tell her I am a doctor and you are here and get her to come with me.'

As she was saying this Maw came out of the doors again on her own with a tobacco pouch and started rolling a fag and Peppa jumped up and before I could stop her she ran out onto the lawn and sprinted towards Maw and she shouted 'Maw! It's us!'

I stood up. Maw was standing on the patio with her mouth open and her hands out and Peppa ran up to her and hugged her and Maw nearly fell back. She was shouting and clinging onto Peppa and then Peppa started pulling her hand and dragging her back towards us. I stepped out of the trees and walked towards them and Maw saw me and I waved and she made a big crying sound like 'AAAH!' and let Peppa pull her. I ran over and she got me and hugged me hard and she was crying and going 'Oh Sal. Oh Sal . . .'

We pulled her into the trees and she was shaking and swaying like she was going to faint. Peppa was going 'You can come with us. We live in the wood with Ingrid and you can come and live with us. We made you a bender.'

Maw said 'What? I can't. Wait, I can't . . .'

And then she saw Ingrid and Ingrid stepped up to her and took her face in her hands and said 'You are saved by us. You can come with us and we will look after you.'

Maw was shaking still and she said 'Where are we going?' and we started pulling and dragging her back through the woods. It was like she was blind and couldn't see where she was and we had to pull and hold her hand and go 'Come on, that's it, come on, just up along here . . .' As we got near the wall I heard a voice shouting 'Claire? Claire?'

We got her over the wall and I ran in front and dragged all the branches off the Rolls-Royce and Ingrid got down under the steering wheel with her bit of wire again. Peppa pulled Maw up to the car and when she saw it she looked around and said 'It's a Rolls-Royce' and Peppa said 'Aye, we nicked it.'

I opened the back door on the lane side and we got Maw in and I made her lie down by the seat where your feet go and Peppa covered her in a blanket and then jumped in. Ingrid was shouting in German at the car and then it started and she went 'Aha!'

Ingrid backed off the grass and then roared off fast up

the lane and I was in the front seat looking back to see if anyone came after us. We drove a bit up and then Ingrid swung the car round in a driveway and went back down the lane past the Abbey entrance and started going fast and we got rocked and swayed about going round the corners. Peppa was saying to Maw 'You stay there Maw and then nobody can see you.'

On the other road Ingrid slowed down a bit. It was starting to get dark again but there was nothing following us. We got back down and turned right onto the main road and just cruised along and Maw sat up on the back seat. She just looked amazed and kept crying and then laughing and hugging Peppa. She said 'I thought you were dead' and she cried again.

Her hair was nice short. It was dyed blond and she was still really pretty and looked young and her eyes were clear and bright even though she was crying. I sat in the front seat looking back at her.

She said 'Where did you go?'

I said 'We ran and we survived in the forest. And we met Ingrid.'

Peppa said 'She's German. She taught me how to say arse in German and it's just like arse in Scottish.'

Maw said 'Everyone's looking for you. I thought you were dead. The polis told me they thought you might be dead. They thought someone had got you . . .'

I said 'Nobody got us. We escaped and hid in the woods.'

Then Maw leant forwards and put her hands round my face and said 'Sal I'm sorry.' And she started crying.

I said 'I'm not sorry I killed Robert Maw.'

Maw said 'Oh Sal' and kept on crying.

We were getting back near the Little Chef and I said to Ingrid 'What're we going to do with the Rolls-Royce?'

And she said 'We leave it. In a layby near and I will leave money in it for the window and the petrol for the owner.'

Maw said 'Where are we going? I was in the rehab and . . .'

Peppa said 'Maw you are gonna come and live in the woods with us. We've got a camp and we have a fire at night, it's great.'

I said 'Maw you cannae drink.'

She said 'Sal I'm sober. I've stopped. I'm gonnae stay stopped. Oh Sal . . .' And she cried again for a bit. And then she said 'This is mad.'

Peppa said 'Maw have you got any fags?' and Maw said 'Aye, roll-ups' and Peppa said 'Geez one' and Maw laughed and said 'No Peppa' and I said 'No Peppa.' Then Maw said 'I'm giving them up too.'

We pulled into a layby about half a mile from the Little Chef and there was nobody around. Ingrid pulled the wire out from under the steering wheel and the car stopped and the lights went off. It was dark and Ingrid got a notebook out of her pocket and pulled out a piece of paper from it and wrote 'Thank you for this car and here is money to pay for the window' and then she put a roll of tenners in the note and folded it and left it on the front seat. She said 'I left a hundred pounds. Windows in this car are very expensive.'

We left the blankets in the car and Ingrid went in front with a head torch and I went at the back with one and we climbed over a wall and went across a field and got into the woods behind it. Maw had Converse on and they were okay for walking, not like the heels she used to wear a lot when she was stripping. She did okay going along through the woods and sometimes she went 'Oooh it's spooky' and she laughed. We climbed up a bit and followed a path along a high bit and we could see the Little Chef lights down below through the trees. Then we found the path towards the top of the valley where the river was and where we climbed up. None of us spoke, we just climbed up through the woods and there was just the sound of our feet on the snow and twigs. There was a wee bit of moonlight from a half moon and the stars were out already and they were bright.

Peppa was holding Maw's hand and watching her as we started down the other side and saying 'Careful there Maw' and 'Just a wee step there' and I knew she liked it leading her and showing her where we were going.

Ingrid was going slower than she normally did and holding her back and then she stopped and bent and let out a long low moan. I went over to her and put my hand on her and she said 'Bad pain Sal.'

I said 'We've got more painkillers at the camp' and she shook her head and in the moonlight her face was all screwed up and she had her teeth clamped together. Maw said 'Is it your back darlin'?' and Ingrid nodded her head up and down and then let out a big long breath. She straightened up and said 'Come. We go. I will go at the back. I go slow.'

I gave Peppa my head torch and she led Maw and I walked behind with Ingrid holding her arm and she was gripping my hand hard. It took ages to get back to the camp and I had to push Ingrid up the slope and she was in agony all the way.

We got into the camp and I got the fire going and we lit Ingrid's candles and then got her sitting by the fire and got a blanket for her and I put some rocks in the fire to warm. I got her two ibuprofen and codeine and she said 'No. All of them' and she took all six left in the pack.

Peppa got the head torch and showed Maw her bender and Maw was going 'Did you make this? It's great. Oh a wee table!' Peppa was really excited about Maw having a bender and then she brought her and sat her by the fire and wrapped her in a blanket and I made tea for all of us. Ingrid just sat in the firelight with a kind of grin on her face.

We had corned beef and beans and bread and then we had some Dundee cake and then Maw rolled a fag and lit it. She looked young and pretty in the firelight and I sat next to her and she put her arms round me and Peppa. Ingrid said 'Claire may I have a cigarette please?' I didn't know Ingrid smoked, and she was a doctor, but Maw rolled her one and she lit it and coughed a bit and said 'I have not smoked a cigarette for forty years. But it is a special night. It reminds me of being young. In the DDR everyone smoked.'

Peppa said 'Ingrid is really old Maw. She's seventy-five.'

And Maw said 'Never!'

'And she's a doctor and she defected from the DDR in nineteen seventy-nine. And she was a hippie and got beaten up by the polis on the hippie convoy' I said.

Peppa said 'And she loved a man called Max and he cheated on her and she got depressed and did research. And she had a boyfriend called Matt who was young enough to be her son. And she knows all the German swear words.'

Ingrid was laughing. 'I have told them my whole life Claire. I have never told my whole life to anyone before.'

Maw laughed too. Then she said 'I am so sorry. You've had to look after them.'

Ingrid said 'They look after me. They are angels. They have made me happy.'

Peppa said 'I'm an angel' and held her hands together like she was praying and put on a holy face.

Maw said 'Are you really a doctor?'

Ingrid said 'Yes. I was in general practice for fifteen years before I retired and came to live here.'

Peppa said 'Ingrid can make bread and candles. And she can sew hats and make pots and she took three pike teeth out of my hand when I got bitten by a pike I caught with Sal at the other loch, I had a fever and I was really sick and she made me better . . .'

Maw said 'You got bitten by a pike?'

Peppa said 'Aye he was a big bastard an' all, and he ripped three big cuts in my hand. Sal ate him.'

Ingrid said she needed to go to sleep and I wrapped a hot stone for her and went with her over to her bender and she got took off her big coat and boots and then got into the bed and I put the stone in behind her back. She touched my face and said 'We got your mother Sal.' And I kissed her and left her to sleep.

Maw told us what happened when we ran. She woke up hungover like usual and she needed the toilet and she couldn't get out of the room. She banged and called us and Robert for ages and then she started shouting out of the window and banging on it. She found her phone and she tried Robert's and heard it ringing through in the front room. Then she tried our phones and they were dead and she tried two lassies from the club but they didn't answer. She couldn't think who to ring and then she found Ian Leckie's number in her call history and she rang him.

He said he'd come. When he got to the flat he rang and said he'd have to break the door in and she said okay. She knew there was something wrong and then heard the door go in and Ian calling her round the flat and then he went 'Jesus!' And then he started shouting for me and Peppa and he found the key on the carpet and unlocked her door and said 'Don't go in Sal's room Claire' and she thought we were dead or hurt and she screamed and pushed past him and ran in and saw Robert dead on my bed.

Ian called the polis and they came and loads of them piled into the flat and they kept Maw in the front room and kept asking her where we were and she said she didn't know. She couldn't even remember what had happened the night before and she wanted a drink but they wouldn't let her have one.

All the flat got taped off and they started asking everyone in the close if they'd seen us and Ian Leckie and some other men started searching around the flats and the play park and the back of the railway. They took Maw to the station in town and kept asking her what happened and what we did the night before. They asked her all about Robert and they said they'd found nicked phones and cards and drugs in the flat. They kept her overnight and they interviewed Ian Leckie and took his phone and the next day a woman from social services came to see Maw and a solicitor, and Maw was rattling and dying because she needed a drink to cope with it all.

Maw saw a doctor and then they took her into a hospital and gave her a room and pills to calm her down and the polis stayed with her and kept asking her stuff about us. Then the polis said she had to go and talk to the press and she got took to the station and she cried in front of all the cameras and reporters and said for us to come home.

Then they arrested Ian Leckie and questioned him for two days on suspicion of killing Robert. They let him go because they had no evidence on him. Which shows how fucking stupid the polis are.

Maw stayed in the hospital for three more days and all the time they were coming and talking to her and telling her we were still not found. They asked loads about Robert and they told her he had convictions for being a paedo before he met her. She cried and cried and wanted to kill herself. They asked all about Peppa's da and all about my da and all about the club where she worked and the lassies she knew there. The doctor and the social workers kept coming in to her and telling her stuff and examining her. And then the solicitor came to see her and told her she wasn't being charged with anything yet. But they might charge her later with neglecting us. The doctor said she needed to go into a rehab because she was having withdrawals and shaking all the time. The doctors said they would pay and Maw said it cost £2,000 a week.

After we'd been away a week they told her she was going to a rehab. Some lassies from the club and Ian Leckie came to see her and she had a long talk with him and started telling him about what she'd been like when she was drinking. He said that we'd be found safe and she needed to go into the rehab. The polis wouldn't tell her anything about the search for us or where they thought we were.

Ian brought her some clothes and the long grey coat to go to the rehab in and he gave her fags. The polis kept her phone.

She got driven down to the rehab by two social workers and a polis woman who told her they thought I'd killed Robert. Maw knew I'd killed Robert. When she got to the rehab she had to be searched for drink and drugs and then she got a room with another lassie called Jackie. By then she hadn't had a drink for seven days.

Jackie was the woman we saw her with on the lawn and she was a hairdresser and she cut Maw's hair and dyed it while they were going to lots of meetings and having talks with the doctors. The polis came to see her after three days and told her they hadn't found us and asked her loads of questions about us again.

Maw stayed off the drink and started to get better and she talked to people about what she had been like with us, and about Robert, and she cried a lot. Ian Leckie drove down to see her for a day and she talked to him for a long time and he told her she was doing the right thing. She said she stayed sober by not drinking for one day at a time and by being honest. She said it was simple but it wasn't easy.

On that first night we all slept in our bender and while Peppa was getting undressed Maw looked at all our survival stuff like the sleeping bag and the kettle and the fire steel. I showed her the head torches in case she wanted a pee. She said 'Where did you get it all?'

I said 'I bought most of it online. I nicked some things too.'

Maw picked up the rucksack and held it out in front of her. 'How did you pay for it?' she said.

'I nicked money off Robert and I nicked the cards he got.'

She said 'You were planning it for a long time weren't ye?'

I said aye and she sighed.

I said 'I've still got some money left. Look. Fifty quid. We can use it for food.' I pulled the notes out of the zipper pocket in the rucksack and she stared at them.

Maw said 'I still haven't seen you smile Sal.'

Peppa shouted from the bed 'Ah'm the only one can make her smile. And she laughs too sometimes. She laughs if I say Ah'm gonnae have ginger pubes.'

I didn't laugh then though and Maw looked sad.

She took off her coat and her Converse and got in with Peppa and I got in too.

It was a bit of a squash with all three of us but it was nice and warm. We were all really tired and I started telling them about the French Revolution and when they were chopping off the heads of all the posh people and then started chopping off everyone's head in 1793 when they did the Terror and a lawyer called Robespierre who thought they needed to kill everyone who didn't want the revolution.

Maw listened and then she whispered 'Where did you learn all that stuff Sal?'

And I said 'Online.'

Maw lay awake for a long time and I lay listening to her breathing. I was glad we'd got her and she was sober and I started to relax. Peppa was in between us.

Chapter Fifteen

Frost

In the morning Maw was gone.

I felt her get up in the night and get the head torch and put on her coat and Converse. I thought she was away for a pee. I lay next to Peppa waiting for her to come back and I fell back asleep. When I woke up it was getting light and Maw wasn't there.

It was raw cold again and even the embers on the fire had frost on them. It was still, with no wind and the frost was like white fur on everything. I got my fleece on and stood and listened outside the bender. Maw had left a track in the frost, up to the latrine and then back along. I could see her tracks go past Ingrid's and then away down into the wood. I stood and listened and my breath made stiff white clouds around my head. It was so silent I could hear my blood.

Waiting there by the cold fire to hear something I tried to plan. Hunters try to predict the behaviour of prey, so they know where and when they will be, they know what they want like water and food and they adapt their behaviour. Predators exploit the needs of prey and try to get them where they are most vulnerable, like doing the toilet or feeding.

I knew Maw wouldnae be out for a walk and I knew she wasn't at the latrine. I went across and looked at the tracks going by Ingrid's. The Converse had left imprints in the frosted grass and the tracks were deep like she was stamping. A new fluff of frost was forming on the indentations so I knew they'd been there for an hour or so. The tracks were erratic too, going one way and then adjusting the line she took towards the wood. It was still dark when she left and she was following the beam of the head torch.

I felt cold and flat and calm and I went into our bender and whispered to Peppa 'Ah'm going for a walk wi' Maw. When you get up boil water and make Ingrid some pine tea and porridge. We'll be back in a couple of hours.'

She stirred and murmured 'alright' and went back asleep. I checked she was warm and pulled the covers up around her.

The money was gone from the rucksack pocket. I got my knife and the airgun and the monocular. I put the first aid kit in the backpack with some paracord and a bag of raisins.

Once the fire was going and stacked up I went to see Ingrid. She was sitting up on her bed with a quilt around her. She smiled when I came in and I said 'Maw's gone.'

She said 'Oh Sal.' She was breathing hard.

I said 'Ah'm going to find her. She's left tracks. Peppa'll get your breakfast.'

Ingrid said 'She will come back to you.'

And I looked her hard in the eye then and said 'No she won't.'

At the top of the woods her tracks were easy to follow, she was stamping and blundering and there were scuffed leaves and broken twigs. She was going down towards the badgers and the wee valley where the river was. I tracked her between the trees and she made a big loop to start with so she was heading up the river away from the best crossing place. I could see dents in one place where she'd fallen and gone onto her knees, and the leaves and needles were swept out dark by her big coat. The sun was breaking in between the trees above the freezing mist but as I went down into the valley it got thicker and the ground was bristly white with frost.

I saw where she crossed the river. There was cracked ice and a footprint in the mud and she'd slipped by some rocks and there was a big triangle swept out of the frost and scrabbling marks where she tried to get up. There was a handprint in the leaf mould.

The track got less easy to follow past the badgers and the trees and she'd found the path we followed the night before so there were our tracks too but they were frosted more than hers so I could tell which were which. I kept stopping and listening.

She had stopped at the top of the first big bank and had a fag by a birch tree. There was a roll-up butt squashed into the dirt and smears of a muddy hand on the white bark.

I was starting to feel excited. We all leave tracks of where we've been but some people leave tracks that are easier to follow. Because I could now predict where she was headed, along the path towards the road and the Little Chef I went out wide and sprinted up and through the thicker trees. Maw wasn't as fit and fast as me and I thought I could make up her start and cut her off before she got to the road. I knew where she was going and I knew why. She had the money.

I had to climb up and run through Scots pine always

looking and listening down to my right for where the path ran. When I got to the top the sun had broken the mist and was glinting off the top of the pines and then away down to the path it was still flat and misty.

I was trying to figure out how far she could've got. If she'd got to the road she could go up to the Little Chef. I didn't know if they sold drink or if she could get it first thing in the morning. But alcoholics will always find a way to get it if they want it. You can't trust them. If they say they've had one they've had ten. If they say they've had none they've had twenty.

I came up to the top above the Little Chef, the dropping down to the path was a sheer cliff about ten metres to the bottom there. I could see the car park where we nicked the Rolls-Royce. I crept down along the edge of the drop going from tree to tree. I heard her before I saw her and it was sobbing. It came through the mist like a dry cough and echoed. I flattened onto the ground and crawled towards it.

She was sitting ghost grey against a tree on the edge of the drop and convulsing like she was being sick and the sound of her sobs rang across the woods. I crawled till I was about fifteen metres from her and lay watching from behind a frosted tussock. I got the gun and levelled it and set the bead into the V on the back sight on her head and waited.

She was still now and I had my finger on the trigger and it was pumped ten times and there was a pellet in the breach. At that range it would go through 9mm plywood on ten pumps. I couldn't see the detail of her face with one eye closed and the bead focused on the grey blob that was her through the mist.

I breathed in and waited with her in the sight. I thought about her and the days and nights since I was wee when she was asleep or out of it. My jaw was clenched tight and ached, and cold was pricking me where I lay on the ground.

Then I shouted 'MAW.'

She turned her head and I took my eyes off the sight and saw her face. Her mouth was open and she was dribbling snot and her eyes were pink. She called in a tiny voice 'Sal?'

I shouted 'YOU LEFT US. YOU LEFT PEPPA.'

She creased up her face like she was hurting and hacked out a sob and it echoed.

I shouted again. 'YOU LEFT HER MAW. SHE CAME AND GOT YOU AND YOU LEFT HER.'

She stood up slowly looking around her and she moved slow. I kept the gun on her. She shouted 'Sal I'm sorry. I'm sorry.'

I started to stand and she saw me up above her and turned towards me with her hands out. I shouted 'Did ye take the money?' and she nodded and tears were dripping off her chin and down into the frost. She put her hand in her pocket and took it out and held the notes up. She stepped nearer the drop in front of her down to the path and the Little Chef.

I took a step forwards with the gun on her still. She was standing on the edge by the big tree but looking back up at me. I started to see her more clearly as I walked down through the mist. Her face was screwed up and her eyes were closed and soaked with tears and mist. I kept the gun on her. My heart was beating hard. 'Were ye going for a drink?' I said.

She turned so as not to look at me and staggered and nodded again and her body convulsed into a sob. Then she stepped forwards and walked off the edge.

There was cracking twigs and a grunt and then a thud and rustling. I dropped the gun and ran to the edge of the cliff and looked down. She was on her side with the big coat spread out round her like a skirt on the white frost. She was still. One arm up like she was pointing and one arm back behind and her legs were twisted together.

My heart started banging faster and faster and a tight knot clenched up in the centre of my chest and sweat burst out of my forehead. I staggered dizzy backwards and felt sick coming in my belly and chest. I clung onto the tree to stay up and tried to breathe and felt the breaths stick in my throat and not go in. I hung there against the tree feeling the ridges of the bark on my fingertips, finally got a breath in and held it. The sweat was freezing onto my face but my chest was burning. I fell with my face into the bark of the tree and the ridges and dents pressed into my skin. I stayed there like that not breathing with my arms round the trunk to keep me up. When I took in a breath I breathed in the tree and the bark scratched my lips. Things were starting to go black with just wee flashes.

Then I heard a man's voice shout 'Sal?' and then shout it again. I stayed by the tree and I heard feet running on the path below and then he said 'Christ! Are you okay? Stay there. Sal? Sal?'

I let go of the tree and crawled to the edge and looked down.

Adam was standing over Maw and he looked up. He said 'I saw you up there from the car park. I saw her fall.' He knelt by Maw and he had his hand on her forehead and he was feeling her neck. He looked up again. 'I think she's concussed. She needs to sit up.'

I got up then and ran down the long slope through the trees to the path and then back up, and sprinted to where Maw was. Adam had her sat up and she was moving her head and blinking. He was holding her face and looking into her eyes and going 'You're okay. Can you hear me? What's her name?'

I said 'Claire.'

He said 'Claire . . . you fell and you've had a shock. Can you hear me?'

Maw's eyes rolled a bit and then she shook her head and said 'Sal.'

Adam said 'Sal's here.'

Then Maw's head flopped back and her eyes rolled and Adam took the weight of her head. He was patting her face gently. Her face was soaked and smeared with dirt and her head looked like it was too heavy for her neck. Adam was going 'Claire . . . Claire . . .' in a soft voice.

He was wearing a blue fleece and jeans and he pulled the fleece off and wrapped it round Maw's shoulders. He had a T-shirt on underneath and his arms were thick and muscly but he was really gentle the way he held her face. He turned to me. 'She's in shock. It's pretty soft here where she fell. I think the wind's just knocked out of her. I was coming back to my car and I looked up and saw her fall and then I saw you. I knew it was you.'

There was a pile of frosty leaves all sprayed round her where she'd hit the ground. If Peppa was there she'd have said it was a good job she landed on her arse. I said 'She's my maw. We were walking and she didn't see the edge.'

He said 'Easily done in the mist.' Maw looked like she had gone to sleep. Adam looked at me and he looked worried. He said 'I'll lie her back down.'

I said 'You could slap her. It might wake her up.'

But he started to lower her down really gently and he said 'There doesn't look like there's a head injury. She's breathing.'

I said 'Get her in the recovery position.'

He let her lay back and then he got her behind the knee and pulled it up and then turned her onto her side. Then her eyes opened and she jerked and opened her mouth and retched like she was being sick but nothing came out. She breathed in again deep and said 'Sal' again.

I said 'I'm here Maw.'

Her eyes were shut but she was breathing harder and Adam pulled the fleece out from under her and covered her. She lay like that for a few minutes breathing hard on her side with her eyes closed and then she suddenly opened them and said 'Jesus. What did I do?'

Adam said 'You fell . . . from up there.'

She said 'Sal . . .'

She started shifting and Adam helped her sit up. She sat up slowly and stretched her face, opening her mouth wide like she was gulping. She opened her eyes wide and looked up at me.

Adam squatted down next to her and started squeezing her legs. Maw went 'Ow' and jumped a bit. Her face was all smeared and red from crying but she was looking at Adam. He held his finger in front of her face and moved it and her eyes followed it. He said 'How many?'

She said 'One.'

He said 'How many of me?'

She said 'One' and smiled.

Adam held her face again and looked into her eyes and then he felt her arms and pulled her fingertips and said 'Feel that?'

Maw said 'Aye.'

Then he said 'Tell me your name' and Maw said 'Claire Brown' and Adam said 'What are your daughters called?' and

Maw said 'Salmarina and Paula. But we call them Sal and Peppa.'

Adam looked round at me and said 'How is Peppa?'

I said 'She's fine aye. She's back at the camp with our nanna.'

Maw said slowly 'Do you know each other do you?'

Adam said 'We met up by the stones on the frozen loch. I was skiing. Yes I know Peppa. You don't forget Peppa' and he laughed and his eyes went wide and sparkled and I thought how beautiful he was.

He helped Maw up and he said 'Where does it hurt?' and Maw said 'Ma arse' and he laughed again. 'You were lucky, that's quite a drop.'

Maw said 'I am really hungry. I am so hungry.' She looked at me and then pulled me in and cuddled me and I said 'Don't say sorry' and she had her mouth buried in my neck and she said 'I won't.' She pressed the money into my hand.

We walked across to the Little Chef and Maw limped a bit and kept clutching at her back. Adam told us he was going back to uni and he'd stopped for breakfast and he saw us when he was coming out to his car. It was quiet in the café and we got a booth on the far side where I could see the door. Me and Maw both ordered a big breakfast and Adam had coffee.

He told Maw 'You need to be careful in case you've got concussion. If you feel sick or feel like you're going to black out you should really see a doctor.'

I said 'It's okay. We know a doctor.'

Adam asked me how old I was and I told him and he said 'Wow. You look older.' And I felt my face getting red. Maw put her hand on my head and said 'Nah. She's still a bairn' and I said 'Am not' and Adam laughed.

Maw went to the toilet and I sat with Adam for a bit

and then I said 'Adam don't tell anyone you met us right? We're not supposed to be here and there's someone after us and we need to hide in the woods for a bit. Don't tell anyone about us.'

Adam said 'I won't. Who's after you? I could help you.'

I said 'Nah we're safe. We just need left alone. I look after them, Maw and Peppa. I've got a knife and I can protect them. I'm not scared of anything.'

Adam looked straight at me and said 'No I don't think you are. You *are* an outlaw then.'

And I said aye and he smiled at me and said 'I can't believe you're only thirteen' and he got up to go as Maw got back and she said thank you to him and shook his hand and he told her to see a doctor.

We watched Adam drive off out of the car park in a little blue car with a roof rack with skis on it. Maw said 'He's bonny Sal so he is.'

I said 'Peppa fancied him.'

Maw said 'I fancy him' and she laughed.

Then she held my hands across the table and said in a quiet voice 'I got too hungry and I got too angry and I got too lonely and I got too tired. And I got too scared. And when I'm scared I run. And I was running to find somewhere to blot it all out Sal, that's what I've always done. When I saw you and Peppa and what you'd done and why you'd done it I just wanted to run and blot it all out.'

Her face was soft and her eyes were bright again. She had no make-up on and she'd washed her face in the toilets and it shone.

She said 'I thought you were going to shoot me.'

I said 'I was. I will again if you leave Peppa.'

She sighed hard and picked up my hands and kissed them. We paid and I bought some ibruprofen from the wee shop for Ingrid and we got milk. We started back up and I ran up to the top of the ridge above the Little Chef and got the gun. We went on the path up towards the valley and we went slow because Maw said her legs were sore.

Maw told me about when she was wee. She was fostered to an old couple called Cliff and Mary because her maw couldn't look after her and she never saw her and she didn't know who her da was. Cliff told her her da was a gangster. Cliff and Mary were alright but they were old and she thought they only fostered her for the money and they never adopted her. She wanted to find her maw one day she said and see what she was like and if she was still alive. They lived on a scheme of new houses and they had a garden and garage and they went to the kirk. Maw said she liked the kirk and Sunday school and she learned the bible and they went on holiday to Spain one year when she was about eleven. Cliff did electrics for the council and Mary was a dinner lady in the school.

She met my da at school. He was a year older than her and his name was Jimmy but everyone called him Maz. Maw said she hated school and she was thick and she plunked it most of the time. She used to go to the park and drink and smoke weed with kids from school. She said the first time she drank she felt brilliant. She said it was like someone had turned all the lights on in the world.

She said 'I'm not clever like you Sal. I don't know anything. I don't even know how to stay sober.'

I said 'Just don't drink. Not even one.'

She said aye and we crossed the river and she had a rest on a rock and had a fag and I looked for ash saplings because I wanted to make a bow and I was going to laminate it. I cut one about the width of my wrist.

We started back towards the camp and the sun was up

high and starting to melt the frost and snow. I told Maw not to say to Peppa about Adam or about her running down to the Little Chef and Maw said she wouldn't.

When we got back to the camp Ingrid was sitting by the fire with a blanket round her and carving a bit of wood and teaching Peppa German. Peppa was sharpening thin sticks with her new knife.

She said 'Ah'm making arrows Sal for if you get a bow. Will they work?'

I looked at them and said they'd need flights and the end would need a weight to make it go straight and she said 'The German for arrow is Pfeil. They have a P and an F together in some words, like the word for Pepper, not my name, the stuff they put in haggis, has got a P and an F, it's Pfeffer and you say it pffeffer, so my name would be Pffeffereppa. Why have different countries got different words for everything?'

I said I didn't know. And I didn't but it was a canny question. Maw sat next to Ingrid and Ingrid put her arm around her and said 'Okay?' in a quiet voice and Maw nodded but then she started crying.

Me and Peppa watched her. I'd seen her cry a lot and it didn't upset me but it made Peppa look worried. She said 'Maw do you want to go and see the Goddess called Cheryl?'

Maw laughed and said okay. Ingrid took some of the ibruprofen and went back to her bender to sleep and then we went up through the woods towards the moor and Magna Bra. I left the gun back at the camp but I brought the monocular and my knife. I took the backpack with the raisins and the paracord and I filled a bottle of water from the kettle in case we got dehydrated.

On the way up Peppa talked all the time and I walked behind them. She told Maw all about what Ingrid said about the Goddess and about Ingrid being wee in Berlin and losing her maw and living with Klausi and Hansi. She told Maw loads of German words and all the swear words and Maw laughed at them and kept saying 'Peppa!' when she swore.

The snow was soft at the start of the moor up towards the stones and we saw a Buzzard. As we climbed the snow got thicker and in some places it was blown into ridges that were iced on top in the wind. The wind got up and was stiffer the further up we got and it was a northerly and cold. We all sat in the lee of a drystane dyke and ate the raisins and drank water and looked back down at where we'd come from and you could see our prints in the snow. The wind was making clouds skid along and they made big grey shapes that flew across the snow. Then Maw said 'What's that?' and pointed.

Just below us about fifteen metres away there was a snow ridge and sitting in against it was a white hare with black ears. We all sat still and I watched it through the monocular. I said 'It's a mountain hare. It's gone white for winter.'

It was sniffing and its nose was twitching but its ears were flat and it didn't look bothered by us at all. Peppa said 'Don't kill it Sal' and I said 'Ah'm not going into kill it.' Even though it would be good to eat and the skin would make a good hat.

Maw said 'He's sweet.'

The hare just sat and looked at us and then scraped a bit under its front feet. It was a big one, much bigger than a rabbit, and through the monocular I could see it still had some tufts of grey hair in amongst the white. Its eyes were yellow and it had long lashes that blinked. When we got up to carry on the hare went rigid and alert and then ran away down away from us into snow ridges and you could see the bottoms of its big wide feet. Maw smiled at me and we carried on climbing up.

At the stones Peppa ran around and around shouting 'Hail Cheryl' and me and Maw looked out at the view across and back down the valley towards the lochs, the lines of forest fading and below them flat fields and the river snaking. The town was hidden by a hill, and far beyond it was a flat bluey-grey smudge that could've been the sea.

Maw said 'It's a big place.'

I said 'It's three hundred and seventy-nine square miles total area. You can see it from satellites in space because there is no light pollution. It's just a dark patch in the southwest of Scotland above the Solway Firth.'

Maw felt the top of the stone she was leaning on. It had ice across the top and the lichen looked like it was under glass. She turned and watched Peppa running around the stones. She said 'Does Peppa know about what Robert was doing?'

I said 'A bit.'

She sighed and held my hand and squeezed it. Peppa ran up to us and said 'Ah'm hungry' and we turned and went back down. On the way back Peppa told Maw about Adam the skier. She said 'He was lush Maw, and he made Sal go red.' Maw looked back at me and smiled and I smiled back.

Peppa raced off down the hill towards our woods and Maw walked next to me. She said 'You know I told him your real names.'

I said 'I know. He won't tell.'

Back at the camp Ingrid was asleep and I made rice and beans and corned beef for tea while it got dark. We made food for Ingrid but she didn't want it and Maw went and sat with her and they talked for a bit while I shaved the ash poles down and Peppa read her book with her clip lamp.

Maw said she'd sleep in her bender and we put a hot

stone in a towel to make the bed warm and Peppa went to bed and Maw did too, but I sat up by the fire and watched Maw's bender till it was late and I heard owls screeching.

Chapter Sixteen

Mist

In the morning I checked Maw was still in her bender then got my fleece on and started the fire while they all slept and the sun was just coming up. I boiled the kettle and made Ingrid some pine tea with sugar in it and took it to her bender. She was fast asleep and I left it by her bed.

I put Maw's Converse by the fire because they were damp and then I got the gun and my monocular and went off to have a look around and try to shoot a rabbit. I climbed along the ridge at the top above the camp all past the spruce trees and followed it along where there was nearly a sheer drop down on the side into the woods at the bottom. Then I found a twisty path going down and climbed and slid down into a dip where there were hazel trees with lots of poles and straight sticks coming out. These are good for making arrows if you make a bow and arrow like I saw Ray Mears do once. I went further along and found a wee house all broken down with trees growing out of it. There was a wall made of stones and a bit of a chimney. On the other side was a wider path going on into more woods and I walked along it. It was an old forestry track leading down but there were no tyre tracks on it.

There was a clearing further down and sheer rock walls all around it and big flat stones lying about in it, covered in thin snow and frost. I saw a flash of a rabbit tail running away across it and hid down behind a pine tree. I sat and waited and got out the monocular slowly. Across the clearing under the rock walls there were rabbit holes. One had new mud outside and I scanned across and saw one just sitting near it. A big one. Its ears were straight up and I could see the whiskers twitching. Then two more hopped up next to it. Then another came out of the hole and there were four all just sitting. The big one started scraping at the snow and a smaller one hopped up next to it. It hopped away coming towards me and then turned and watched the other three. They started scraping and pushing at the snow and they were nibbling at grass underneath. The big one just sat with his ears up. He hopped further away then, still towards me, and sat again. He was watching the others and keeping lookout. The other three were hopping along, scraping and nibbling, and he just sat.

Then really far off a dog barked. The big rabbit stamped his back legs three times – bang bang bang – and all four of them shot off towards the hole and vanished.

I sat where I was and the dog barked again. I got up and I was glad I hadn't shot the rabbits. I didn't want to kill those rabbits.

I climbed up through the woods again and got to the top of the ridge and followed it along to the top of the sheer cliff that looked down on the clearing. You could see the forest stretching away down white and grey in the frost and two big stretches of mist like arms lying along the bottom of the valley. In a gap in the mist I could see the road faint between the trees and a tiny grey car went along it and disappeared into the mist. It was quiet then and I sat on the cliff edge looking down at it all. The dog barked and it was even further away like a wee gruff voice shouting 'Arc!'

I sat with my feet hanging over the cliff. I felt filled up with the cold and the silence and started feeling my body go light and numb, first my bum and my legs and then it crept up till I was just looking again from a big empty space out into the silver misty valley. The wee lights started dropping down like raindrops across it and I was hanging there peering out at them. They formed little lines and zigzags that danced across the view in front of my eyes and my eyes were holes and behind them was nothing. Not even me.

A crow brought me back. It squawked right above me in a high Scots pine and then two others started. I don't know how long I had been there but my legs and bum were still numb and I had to stand up and rub them.

Peppa and Maw and Ingrid all flashed in my mind and I started running. I was panicking and my heart was throbbing and I heard a voice in my head start saying 'You can't do it.' It said it again and again in the rhythm I was running, holding the gun down in my left hand and the monocular bashing me in the chest on its strap round my neck. You can't do it. You can't do it. I hammered along the ridge with the forest below me in and out of the big trees slamming my feet down on the frosted snow that chugged under me. You can't do it. You can't do it.

I was heaving for my breath by the time I got to the path that leads down to Ingrid's bit and I flew down it feeling pains stabbing in my chest, dropping onto my heels as I went down and down towards the camp getting whipped by twigs. Two pheasants burst out from the bushes flapping and clattering off away into the wood. I could smell the fire as I got nearer and the voice stopped. I slowed and just walked the last few metres once I got on the flat and jumped the wee burn by the pool and Maw and Peppa were by the fire in blankets drinking tea.

I said 'Where's Ingrid?' and Maw said 'Still sleeping. You alright Sal?' I was still breathing hard and my face felt all flushed and red. I went into Ingrid's bender and felt her forehead and she was warm.

She opened her eyes. She smiled at me. She said 'I'm okay Sal. You don't worry.' I got in with her and cuddled her. She felt light and bony and tiny like a baby. Her hair smelled of smoke and pine.

When Ingrid was asleep again I got out of the bed and went out to the fire. Maw was stirring a pot of porridge and Peppa had bowls and a pot of jam. Maw said 'Sal . . . are you okay?'

I said 'Ingrid's ill.'

Peppa said 'She's got a bad back. She breaks all the wood with her feet and it makes it sore.'

Maw said 'We'll look after her Sal.'

We had the porridge with jam in it and then Peppa said 'I'm going to run' and she went belting off into the wood and I shouted 'Be careful!' But she was gone.

I sat with Maw and she smoked a roll-up. There were still lots of things I wanted to say to her. So I said 'Let's go and watch the badgers.'

Maw said 'Aye alright.' She saw the airgun standing by our bender when she got up and said 'Is that Robert's?' and I said 'Aye. I nicked it and brought it with us.' Maw stared at it for a minute then said 'Come on then.'

I wrote 'Watchin the bagers' in big letters on a flat rock we used as a seat by the fire with an ember and made an arrow with sticks pointing down to the valley below us. Maw said 'She'll see that.'

I got a blanket. The wind was coming northwesterly so we walked down the river a bit before we crossed on some stones. Maw had no problems walking and jumping around in the woods. I thought she might be all girly and worry about getting her feet wet or go on about mud but she was like me. She was strong and she could climb a slope quick and she jumped the stones across the river with her big grey coat swishing and I didn't have to help her. We walked across the flat valley bottom where there was still mist hanging in the trees. The trees were oaks and coppiced hazel and some alder and birch.

I said 'We'll walk up slow and stay downwind and we might see them coming out.' And Maw whispered 'Okay.'

We crept up towards the bank where the sett was and stopped by a big oak about fifteen metres away. There was a big pile of mud and dry grass outside it and tracks in the snow. Badgers are less active in winter but they do come out, especially if they can find unfrozen ground to dig for worms and slugs.

We sat on the blanket just behind the tree where we could see the sett and I pulled the blanket up around us. I showed Maw how to focus the monocular and she watched through it. There wasn't much wind and the sett was a bit faint through the mist but we could see the black of the hole going in against the snow.

Maw lowered the monocular and turned and looked at me. She smiled and said 'Peppa said you got your period Sal.'

I said 'She tells everyone. She thinks it's funny.'

Maw said 'Were you okay?'

I said 'Aye. Ingrid looked after me. I had to burn ma pants. Ingrid gave me painkillers and a hot rock for ma belly.'

Maw said 'I'm sorry I wasn't with you darlin'. It's horrible innit?'

I said 'It was okay. Ingrid said now I was a woman.'

We watched the sett and it was quiet, not even crows or leaves rustling. Nothing moved and Maw just sat next to me staring out across at the sett. Then Maw put her arm round me and we sat like that for ages.

Suddenly a badger's head appeared in the hole with two black stripes down it looking out and Maw went all tense and whispered 'Sal . . .'

It came straight out and stopped and was sniffing and then another one came out behind it and then another. The third one ran out and ran in front of the others and then sat and they all sniffed. The first one was biggest. I had never seen one not on a screen before and they are bigger than you think and they move all smooth and their backs ripple. The two smaller ones started nosing about in the snow and leaves and one of them kept running away and running back to the others like he was wanting to play. The big one sniffed around and then started off on one of the tracks that led almost straight towards us. The other two got behind it and all three came rippling along towards us and Maw grabbed my hand and squeezed it and I looked and she had her mouth open and a huge smile and her eyes were all wide and bright like she was amazed. The three badgers got nearer and nearer our tree and we just sat frozen. They kept on coming and we could hear them scratching along on the snow and see the grey and black hairs on their fur moving and rolling as they walked. About four metres from us the big one stopped and lifted its head up and stared straight at us. It was staring straight into our eyes with the other two behind it with their noses down still sniffing and scraping. The two behind her looked up then and all three were staring at us. I wanted to laugh because their faces looked so startled and they had wee ears sticking up. Maw was letting out a breath really slowly. We sat like that for a while in the silent wood, me and Maw under a tree staring at three badgers.

Then there were thumps and skittering from feet from down towards the river and I knew it was Peppa sprinting through the woods and I turned my head. The big badger turned slowly and trotted back towards the sett with the two others behind. I heard Peppa shout 'Maw! Sal!' and she came running up through the trees towards us. The badgers were gone straight into the sett.

Maw laughed and said 'I cannae believe that!'

I said 'Neither can I. They're usually nocturnal. I think it was a mother and two cubs. The cubs must be nearly a year old, they get born in February.'

Peppa had arrived and heard me say that and she said 'Like me . . . Ah'm born in February' as she skidded into us and we all flopped over in a big pile and Maw went 'Peppa!'

I sat up and pushed Peppa off me and said 'Ingrid would say that was magic' and Maw said 'It was. I've never seen anything like that.'

Peppa was standing up and brushing all the snow and twigs off her and she said 'Did you see them?' and we said 'Aye.'

We got up and shook the blanket out and walked back up and Maw told Peppa about seeing the badgers and Peppa wanted to go back and watch again but I said it was no good now they'd been spooked and we'd have to come at dusk on a night when there was a big moon.

Peppa said 'They wanted to see you Maw.'

'Aye they must've,' Maw said. 'Everyone wants to see me sober.'

Back at the camp Ingrid was still in her bender and we went in to see her and she sat up and told us she was in pain and her lower back hurt. Maw and Peppa got the fire going again and then they went and got more sticks and I boiled the kettle and then went and sat with Ingrid. She was propped up on her bed with blankets behind her and she looked grey and really tired. She didn't want to eat and I gave her the last four ibuprofen and codeine and then gave her pine tea with sugar.

I told her about the badgers and she smiled and said 'I see them a lot in the daytime. They are special ones who like the day. I saw her cubs in June when they were little. They love to play. The big boar comes up into the camp in the summer at night. You want to know where they go in the winter? They go down along the river and dig in the mud and sand and they turn over big stones to get insects and slugs along there. They are very strong animals. They cross the river even when it is cold.'

I said 'Can they swim?'

'Oh yes they are excellent swimmers. In summer the cubs play in the river. I have seen it.'

I said 'Can we show Maw how to make bread?' and Ingrid said 'Yes she must learn.'

Ingrid was too tired to come out so me and Peppa and Maw got all the flour and yeast and the big bowl and we made bread by the fire. Maw kept laughing and saying 'Are you sure this is how you do it?' and I kept going in to Ingrid and showing her the dough and she told me what to do next. Kneading it was hard work and we all three did it in turns and Maw and Peppa threw it back and forwards to each other like it was a ball. While it was rising by the fire I put potatoes in the fire to cook and set the fire going in the bread oven and Peppa told Maw all about her new book which was about a boy and his mother was dying of cancer and every night a monster came into his room and told him scary stories. Maw said it sounded sad but Peppa liked it.

She told Maw the story of *Kidnapped* and told her all the Scots words in it and Maw laughed.

When the bread was risen I scraped all the embers back and we put it in the oven and Maw sat on the ground and watched it cook through the hole. She kept shouting 'It's getting bigger! It's going all brown!' and she got really excited when we got it out and put it on a stone to cool. It looked lovely and it had the nicest smell of anything in the world.

We had to take Ingrid to go to the toilet and we left her there because she said she wanted to be on her own doing it. We helped her back when she called us and then she asked us to heat up water and put it in the big bowl so she could wash. And we lit some of her candles in her bender when the light started going.

Me and Peppa and Maw had potatoes and cheese and bread but Ingrid said she wasn't hungry and she stayed in her bender. After our tea I got the head torch and went into the woods near us and found another good little ash tree and cut a pole out of it about two metres long. Then I sat by the fire and started shaving it down with my knife. I was going to flatten one side and then laminate the two ash poles either side of a bit of spruce with pine resin. I was going to lash it with paracord while the resin went off and then shape the whole thing into a bow. I'd seen it done on YouTube and you have to just keep shaving away and shaping it thin at either end and then getting thicker towards the middle. It was easy to shape wood with a Bear Grylls knife. Laminated wood is strongest, Ian Leckie taught me that.

Peppa read her book with her clip light and Maw went in to see Ingrid. It was quiet with just the sound of the fire. This was what I liked best in the world. Sitting by a fire at night and listening to the sound of it and carving wood. A little breeze started up and it was westerly and warmer.

I could hear Maw and Ingrid talking but not the words and smell fag smoke coming out so they were smoking roll-ups and Ingrid coughed a bit. Maw was in there for ages with me carving and Peppa reading.

Maw went in her own bender and it rained and I worried that it was going to leak on her so I went through to her with the head torch and she was asleep. The spruce was working and there were no drips or anything on the inside and she was warm.

Chapter Seventeen

Fog

The rain had stopped and all the snow was gone, only grey
crescents of ice left in between the rocks and behind the
benders. There was thick white fog so you couldn't even see
the trees from the bender door. I managed to get a bundle
of kindling going as it started getting light and had to use
a lot of the wood from the middle of the stack in the rack
because the wood on the outside was damp. I shaved a dry
stick from the middle for tinder and then got some dry
twigs going. The fire smoked a lot and pumped up into the
fog and hung over the camp in a cloud.

Looking down towards the river from the camp it looked
like a flat white sea and you could hardly see the trees, they
were just grey lines in the fog. There was no wind and little
beads of silver water formed on the spruce on the benders
and on my fleece arms when I was by the fire putting in
sticks. I put two piles of wood by the fire either side to dry
out and got water from the burn.

Maw came out of her bender and went to pee in the
latrine and then ran back to the fire and sat by it in her
grey coat and had a roll-up. I made the tea. We had black

tea with sugar because we had no milk left, UHT or fresh.

Maw sat and got warm by the fire and then she said 'I had a good talk with Ingrid last night Sal. I told her all about us and the flat. And Robert. I told her all about drinking. She knows a lot about it. She's treated people for drinking. Thing is Sal, I can't stay here. And also she can't stay here. And neither can you. And neither can Peppa.'

I said 'Why?'

Maw lit another roll-up and rubbed her forehead. Little dots of moisture were forming all over her coat. 'Look Sal. I know you wanted to hide and survive and you did that and you looked after Peppa because I didn't. I know that and I'm sorry for that. I'm an alcoholic and I can only survive if I stay sober. And, well, the first thing is I need to be with the people who keep me sober.'

I said 'I can keep you sober. There's no drink here.'

Maw said 'I know. I know you want to but you can't Sal. Only I can and only I can with the people I know from the rehab, and Ian. You don't need to keep me sober. I know about what is wrong with me now after the rehab and I can't have you doing everything and looking after me and Peppa all the time.'

I didn't say anything. I got up and got my bow and sat down again with the knife and started shaving it. Maw carried on talking. 'There's something else. Ingrid thinks she is really ill. Really, really ill. She thinks she's got cancer and all the pain in her back is the cancer. She is in bad pain Sal and she needs to go to hospital and get treated properly. She needs proper doctors and medicine.'

I said 'Will she die?'

Maw said 'She will, aye . . . if she doesn't get treated. They can make her better but not here in a bender in the woods.'

I said 'I'm not leaving Peppa. I'm not getting split up from Peppa.'

Maw said 'Look Sal. I don't know what will happen. Right. Look, in rehab I only had to do two things okay? Not drink and be honest. That was it. I just had to not drink and be honest. So I had to face up to and talk about and be honest about all the things I did. All the things I did to you and Peppa. Can you see that Sal? I had to be honest and tell the truth. If you're honest and you tell the truth then you get better. I got better didn't I?'

I got up and walked over to Ingrid's bender and she was sitting up in her bed and she had her eyes closed. I stood and looked at her. She opened her eyes and smiled and said 'I am good.' She rubbed the wee scar on her cheek. I walked back out.

The wind picked up and the trees tops were getting clearer in the valley and starting to sway. The fog was rolling like waves. My heart started up beating fast and I felt hot and red. My chest felt tight and I breathed hard to get it feeling loose. My leg started vibrating and I walked off away from the fire, and I walked a bit further and then I started running.

I heard Maw shout 'Sal!' but I kept on, along the flat bit of the camp and then down and into the trees over clumps of grass and ferns and round boulders. The fog was still thick the further down I went and I was running into it not seeing what was coming, just running and breathing in the damp air. The ground was soaked with wee puddles and streams in the leaves and they exploded water up as I banged through them. I still had my knife in my hand and the blade flashed in the corner of my eye as my arms went up and down running. And I kept on and felt the blood pulsing in my ears in rhythm with my feet slapping down onto the ground.

I got to the river and ran down it and then jumped it where it was thin and went through some sheer rocks and on the other side I ran up into the trees swerving when one came flying at me out of the fog.

Then I stopped.

The noise in my head kept on, the thump thump thump of my feet and blood. I stood still in the fog and breathed it in. I was in a white cave surrounded by it and grey birch trunks. The thumping in my head got less and less. And then it stopped and then I breathed deep and slow and listened to nothing.

The air felt soft and smooth going into my lungs. My skin felt tingly and warm. The words Maw said bounced around inside my head. Sober. Cancer. Can't. Hide. Survive. Honest. Truth. Pain.

Then a dog barked and it was close. And then I heard a voice. A man's voice shouting. Another man's voice. They were flat and sounded dry coming through the fog. Feet and stamping. A bright yellow shape blurred, moving. Crackling and a beep. A voice on a radio and then a flat man's voice saying 'Okay.'

I turned and ran back. The dog barked more. I sprinted and jumped and flew along back across the river and up and whipping past the trees. Towards the top the fog was thinner and my blood was chug chugging in my ears.

I ran up the steepest bit onto the wee path that led along to Ingrid's bit and the fog was clearing more as I got up and ran into the camp and Peppa and Maw were by the fire. When Maw saw me she shouted 'Sal! Put the knife down!' I looked and I still had it. Peppa ran up to me and she had been crying. I hugged her and walked over to the fire. Maw said 'I told Peppa.'

The fog was starting to lift across our camp and everything

was glistening with wet silver drops. I went in to Ingrid and she was sitting up on her bed.

She said 'There are men and dogs in the wood Sal. I can smell them.'

I said 'I know.'

Her face was in a shadow and I stepped in further and knelt down in front of her. She lifted her head and smiled and I saw her big long white teeth and the wee scar on her cheek. She was just staring at me and smiling. After a bit she said 'Something is going to happen Sal. And I don't think you can do anything now. I think you have done everything you can. Sometimes you can't stop things.'

The tears suddenly came out of nowhere but my face stayed the same and they just came out and went down my cheeks. Ingrid put her hand out and touched the top of my head. She said 'You brought me light. Thank you.'

I could feel the warmth from her hand on the top of my head as I got up and went out. I wiped the tears away so Peppa wouldn't see. She was standing by the fire with Maw and she was biting her lip. The fire was starting to go out and it was cold, just a wee wisp of smoke drifting up from it.

I looked around at the three benders – ours, Ingrid's, Maw's and the spruce branch umbrella over the fire and the wood store and the bread oven. There was pants and a T-shirt hung on the paracord washing line, and pots and cups in the big tin bowl by the fire. The gun was leant up outside our bender and the fishing rod was propped against Maw's. The three bits of wood for the bow were shaved and leaning on one of the rocks we used for a seat. Ingrid's tin of pine resin sat next to the cold fire. The air was still and quiet. Maw had her hand on Peppa's shoulder and they were both staring at me.

The helicopter was sudden. We didn't even hear it getting near, it just came up over the trees behind us loud – chop chop chop – so loud you had to shout. It was polis. I could see the guy sitting looking down out of the side talking into a phone and looking down at us. I grabbed Peppa's hand and said 'Run' and Peppa shouted 'Maw!' and we ran and Maw ran after us.

I shouted to Peppa 'Go up. Up to the moor!' and she took off way ahead of us and I followed and Maw followed me shouting 'Sal!'

We climbed up through the woods running in a line, Peppa in front, and she kept turning and looking back at us. Maw was puffing going up the slope and I waited and grabbed her hand and pulled her.

The helicopter stayed over the camp but it went higher and we could see it hovering and it had POLICE on the side. We went into the big Scots pines where the ground was covered in long needles and it squelched and spat water as we ran through it.

I had nothing in my head only 'get away and don't get nicked'. And then 'stay with Peppa' and then 'stay with Maw'. And then Ingrid.

Peppa was up through the pines, and just at the edge of the moor she stopped. Maw and I came smashing through all the branches and we stopped too and we looked out onto the moor. There was still snow in patches and more as it rose up towards Magna Bra and the stones.

Peppa said 'Which way?'

Maw said 'We can't run. They'll get us.'

I just stood looking up towards the stones where the snow was lying in big long thick lines with heather in between. At the top it was almost all white still. In the wind the sun was breaking from under the clouds and sunlight flooded the whole moor for a second and then went and it was grey and dull again. The chop chop chop of the helicopter was still there behind us. I breathed and breathed and thought and tried to stop and plan. I wanted a plan to come. I needed a plan to come. Something small and achievable I could do right now and make a step towards us thriving.

Peppa said 'Which way Sal? They're coming.'

The snow was grey and washed out and I couldn't walk on and the sounds all around me faded to far away. The larch needles under me were yellow and the cold air seemed to stand still under the grey sky. Something was shifting about in me. Something like silence. Something white.

I said 'I'm not leaving Ingrid.'

Maw hugged me and said 'I'm not leaving you' and Peppa said 'Will we get split up?' I said 'No.'

I was still holding the Bear Grylls knife. I looked at it and then chucked it as hard as I could out onto the moor and it disappeared into the heather and snow.

We started walking back down. We went through the Scots pines and then down through the woods and down the big slope. The fog was all blowing away and the sun came out again and everything looked gold in it.

When we came to the ridge above our camp the helicopter was still hovering and there were three polis. One was standing outside Ingrid's bender talking on a radio. One had a dog and it was sniffing all around the camp on a lead pulling him. And one was a woman and she saw us walking back down towards them and spoke into her radio and then walked up to meet us.

Chapter Eighteen

Home

Peppa was dancing round the house in her pants. Maw was on her phone and I was looking out of the window at the wee garden in the front. Peppa had Salt-N-Pepa on YouTube and she was singing and shaking her arse.

It had snowed again and the pots and the wee bench were covered. The garden was white and soft and the sun was just going down.

Maw got off the phone and said 'Ian's coming in five minutes. Peppa get your jeans on and wear your new trainers.'

And Peppa went 'Yo Mom' in an American accent.

Ian Leckie's car pulled up outside and I saw him get out and open the wee gate and come down and I went and opened the door and he said 'Oh Bonny Sal' and hugged me. He hugged Maw and said 'Everything alright?' Maw said 'Aye' and Peppa came running in from our room in her jeans and trainers going 'Ian Leckie Ian Leckie you are specky . . .' and Ian went 'Hello Peppa.'

Maw said 'Come on then. Let's get going, it takes an hour to get there. Sal get your fleece, it's cold.'

I went through to the spare bedroom where I'd left it. There was a bed and Ingrid's rail from the bender with all her clothes and the Chinese jacket. Her boots were all in plastic boxes by the bed.

Peppa sat in the front and me and Maw sat in the back. Social services were paying for the house and we had three bedrooms like our flat and they were all on the same level and no stairs. Ian was coming down all the time and taking us places. He took Maw to meetings and he took me to interviews and meetings with the psychologist and tomorrow he was taking me back up to the court and I'd know how long I was going to get in jail. I was just going on my own with Ian, and Maw was worried about me being lonely. I told her: I had a solicitor, two social workers, an educational psychologist, a police psychologist, a mental health worker and a police liaison officer. And Ian. I wouldn't be lonely.

I had done four interviews with the police and four interviews with psychologists and three with the social workers. Because I knew Maw couldn't get charged I told the police everything from when I thought about killing Robert to when we came out of the woods. I had to tell them about Ingrid nicking the Rolls-Royce because they knew about that anyway and that was how they found us but it took them three days and for the first day they just searched all along the woods at the bottom by the road and didn't come up near where we were. I asked if Adam told on us but they didn't know who he was. The polis who interviewed me were two women and they were nice and not as thick as the men polis.

I had a solicitor called Fiona McKenzie with me all the time and she loved me and she got me bail with conditions. She said it was unusual to get bail in a case like mine but

the court had heard reports from social services and psychologists and I was being made a ward with a guardian.

She kept saying I wasn't going to prison but I'd go to
a secure place for disturbed kids where they took you
canoeing and rock climbing and I thought that would probably be alright. We didn't know how long I'd be there yet
but she said it depended on what I said to the psychologists
and social workers and what the judge thought.

My social workers were called Kathryn and Neal and
they were there all the time too and they interviewed me
a lot about Robert and what happened and I had to point
to dolls if I didn't want to say a word like 'cock' or 'balls'
but I just said them. They asked me all about Maw and I
had to be careful because I didn't want her charged with
neglecting us and I just blamed Robert for everything and
I told them all about Maw not knowing and I said Maw
cooked us food and looked after us and made bread which
was a bit true because she made bread in the woods. They
asked me if I was angry and I said I wasn't but then I got
angry when they started talking about Peppa and what had
happened to her and I said nothing happened to her. I had
a plan and I sorted everything so nothing happened to her
from when she was first born until then.

They asked me all about Ian Leckie and they said he
was getting checked and the judge would make him a
guardian for us and then he could drive us about and look
after Maw with her drinking.

They asked loads and loads about Ingrid and I told them
her life story from the start to when she met us and Neal
kept yawning. I didn't tell them she cuddled us or that I got
in her bender with her and cuddled her or that I kissed her
because they'd think she was an old lezza who was abusing
us. I told them how she looked after us and taught us stuff

and took us to see the Goddess. I told them how she looked after me when I had my period and how she made candles and bread and Peppa's hat and bought me a monocular and it made me cry. I told them I loved her and she was the best person I had ever met in the world.

Kathryn and Neal were nice but they were both wankers. Kathryn had green dyed bits in her hair and a hippie jumper and Neal had white hair and kept yawning and going 'Uh huh . . . uh huh.' He wore walking boots in the town and they were all clean and new. They said they were making a care plan for me and Peppa. I wanted to say I'd already done that, but I didn't.

Peppa was still calling the Goddess 'Cheryl' and she talked about her like she was real and she would do things for you if you prayed to her. If I lost something or Ian couldn't find a parking space Peppa would go 'Just pray to Cheryl and she will provide . . .' I knew she was taking the piss but Ian thought she was serious and he said to me 'Is she really religious?' and I said 'Aye.' Once when Ian first started taking us we couldn't find a space outside the children's panel meeting we had to go to and then Peppa said about praying to Cheryl and a car pulled out just in front of the building and we got his space. Peppa went 'The power of Cheryl . . .' and Ian looked puzzled.

They interviewed Peppa and Maw a lot and they left us all in a room together for hours with board games and books and magazines and Maw said she thought they were watching us to see if she started being a bad mother. But she didn't.

They asked Peppa all about how she got the scars on her hand and she told them about the pike and they kept asking her if she was scared when we were in the forest and she said only of youse getting us.

Ian Leckie went to the polis and social work meeting

with Maw and he told them all about her disease and the way she was getting better and not drinking.

The psychologists asked me how I felt a lot. One kept asking if I was angry with Maw and Peppa and I said no why would I be angry with them? Then he asked me all about killing things and he asked how I felt when I killed something and I said it depends what it is. I told him about killing Robert and I told him about killing rabbits and fish and the grouse. I told him about not wanting to kill a deer after I saw one and about not wanting the kill the rabbits after I saw it warning the others. He said I kept talking about what happened and not how I *felt* about what happened and I said it was the same thing.

Anyway I didn't know how I felt and I still don't know how I feel until I feel bumping and pain in my chest or in my head or until I disappear and watch everything from black space. I didn't tell him any of that. I don't know why everyone is so worried about how they feel. How you feel doesn't really matter. What matters is knowing stuff and doing things.

Peppa was talking German in the car to Ian. She was pointing to all the bits in the car and telling him the German word for it. She had learned a load more German online since we left the forest and sometimes she says sentences in German to me and Maw. If Maw asks her a question she sometimes answers it in German and Maw gets annoyed with her and she goes 'Warum bist du böse Mutti?' which means 'Why are you angry Mummy?' She swears less in English now but much more in German and in the car she started telling Ian German swear words again, and things she said were really rude. And as he drove along she made him say 'Lecken mein Hoden.' And I don't know what that means and neither did Ian but when he said it Peppa nearly pissed herself laughing and she knelt up in the seat and looked back at me and Maw. She was jumping up and down with her eyes all bright and her lovely white teeth.

If the social workers thought she'd been fucked up by Maw and Robert and the flat and not having a da, they should've seen her then, giggling and bouncing about and shouting 'Do ye know what he said?' to me and Maw, and us laughing too even though we didn't.

Kathryn and Neal were wankers but they said one thing that was true and that was that we were staying together and even when I got locked up in the place for disturbed kids, Peppa was staying with Maw and as long as Maw stayed sober we were staying together.

I was fourteen in a week. Peppa said she was going to sing Silent Night in German because my birthday was Christmas Eve but I knew I wouldn't be there after the court tomorrow. So did Maw but she didn't let Peppa see her cry. Maw said Jackie from rehab was going to come and cut her and Peppa's hair when I went up with Ian in the morning. Maw's roots were showing.

Ian started slowing down and looking about and then he saw the sign for the hospice. Snow was falling. We sat in silence in the car in the car park. I couldn't see the entrance clearly because the snow was swirling and dancing and making grey and silver shapes. The light from the entrance was warm and gold and glowed through it. There was a leafless tree, just a wee sapling, in the grass in front with a string of silver lights in it. It was rocking in the wind and blowing snow. Next to it was a pond. The snowflakes were landing on the water and disappearing. White and then gone.

Then we all got out and went in.

Acknowledgements

I am deeply grateful to my beautiful wife Jill without whom I would not have thought of, written or finished this book. She is the best person I have ever met in the world. And equal love and thanks to my wonderful children Jimmy, Molly and Susie. Thank you to everyone in my family, most especially my big brother Jim and his wife Bev, Paddy, Melica, Seth, Sadie, Ezra, Dave and Jenny, Richard and Tamsin, Andrew, Claire and all Welsh Finighans and O'Briens.

Thanks to all the friends who have put up with me and who are too numerous to name, but I will try: John Sexton, Freddie Nolan, Jenny Fraser, Alan McCreddie, Joe McCreddie, Eilidh Cownie, Rupert Crisswell, Kate Gilbertson, Catherine Kerr-Dineen, Zoe Darbyshire, Pete Kill, Trent Baker, John Cheshire, Nick and Nicky Crowhurst and Bob Travis.

Enormous gratitude to my agent Cath Summerhayes and everyone at Canongate Books; Rafaela Romaya, Jenny Fry, Jo Dingley, Rona Williamson, Anna Frame and Vicki Watson for their talent, support and enthusiasm. Thanks also to my copyeditor Alison Rae, my proofreader Lorraine McCann and my cover designer Robert Hunter.